The Disappearance of Inspector Lestrade

Bob Madia

Paperback ISBN 978-1-78705-630-5
ePub ISBN 978-1-78705-631-2
PDF ISBN 978-1-78705-632-9

Published by Orange Pip Books
335 Princess Park Manor, Royal Drive, London, N11 3G
www.orangepipbooks.com

Cover design by Brian Belanger

Dedicated to THE Woman in my life, Dawn; my love forever, a beauty that never fades, a dream come true.

Introduction

I have been a collector of anything involving Sherlock Holmes and his literary agent, Sir Arthur Conan Doyle, since I first read *The Adventures of Sherlock Holmes* when I was twelve years old. I had enjoyed the Basil Rathbone films which were shown alternating weekends during the winter on Channel Nine WGN in Chicago. Opposite them were Charlie Chan mysteries and I humbly admit to liking those more. I thought they were funny.

Anytime there was a new television show, movie, book, magazine or game, I was there. I always tried to be first in line. I always wanted the first copy. I was into Sherlock Holmes before it was cool to be into Sherlock Holmes (thank you Mr. Gatiss and Mr. Moffatt).

When I was young(er), I was the easiest person to shop for when it came to Christmas or my birthday. "Just get me something for my Sherlock Holmes collection," I'd say. Back in the day, it was easy to find something for my collection that I didn't already have. Now, I get more duplicates than surprises, and I'm told it's a challenge to find something I don't already have. What was once a pretty easy task has become a curse for my loved ones who try desperately to find a book I don't already have in my more than 1500 volume collection. "I don't remember seeing this in your collection," they'd say handing me an obviously gift-wrapped tome. I'd open it and the expression on my face would instantly betray the truth of the matter. "You already have it," they'd say, crestfallen. "Sorry, yes," I'd respond. "Let me show you." We'd then go into the "library" and I'd pull the hardcover off the shelf. "Also, here's the paperback version,"

I'd point out from another section. "And here's the Spanish translation, the Braille version and the graphic novel."

Add dozens of toys, games, posters, T-shirts, puzzles, pipes, hats, and varied other knick-knacks and it's no wonder people now say "I never know what to get him. He has everything!"

That's actually not true. There are literally thousands of items and books I don't have, but they're not easily located or purchased. I don't have any of the original Strand Magazine appearances of Sherlock Holmes. I can't afford first editions of the original stories. You just can't walk into a Barnes and Noble and walk out with a first edition of *The Pursuit of the Houseboat* by John Kendrick Bangs. That I found at a Star Trek convention, believe it or not. Oddly, Star Trek conventions are good places to find Sherlockian items to add to a collection. I found homemade buttons or Lt. Cmdr. Data as Sherlock Holmes and Geordie LaForge as Dr. Watson in the Star Trek/Sherlock Holmes crossover episode "Elementary, Dear Data" from *Star Trek: The Next Generation*. I found a copy of the rare first issue of The Paperback Exchange edition of Sherlock Holmes books from editor Gary Lovisi for only a dollar. I was even offered "anything" in a booth in trade for my deerstalker hat. I did not part with it.

Finding new items for my Sherlock Holmes collection has never been difficult for me. Except in one case.

Back in the 1970s there was a TV show called *Ellery Queen*, starring Jim Hutton as the great detective and created by Columbo and Jessica Fletcher creators Richard Levinson and William Link. I loved this show and I read the real Ellery Queen mysteries I found in the local library. I found one book called "A

Study in Terror" in which Ellery is given a handwritten document supposedly done by Dr. Watson and being an unpublished adventure of Sherlock Holmes wherein Holmes hunts Jack the Ripper. The book was in the "free" paperback section of the library and didn't have enough of Ellery Queen in it at the time for me to read it. Since it was in the library, I put it back because I didn't believe in keeping books I got from the public library. A year later I would really get into Sherlock Holmes and I went back to find that book. It was gone. I wouldn't find another copy for more than sixteen years! I searched library book sales, used book stores in the city of Chicago (always a good place to find one or two editions of books to add to the collection), antique stores, and even garage sales. I traveled far and wide searching for a copy of that book (when I say "far and wide" I actually only mean used bookstores in Michigan and Wisconsin as well as Chicago). I just couldn't find one. The story had been reprinted in a collection of Jack the Ripper stories called "Red Jack," but it just wasn't the same as having an original copy.

One day sixteen years after reading the book originally, I was looking up a phone number (in a phone book...remember those?) for a local bookstore and noticed a number for a recently opened used bookstore about ten miles from my house. It wasn't in an area I traveled frequently, however, so I'd never seen the place before locating the phone number.

On my next day off from work, I made the short trip to the store and what do I find on the bottom shelf of the paperback mystery section? TWO copies of "A Study in Terror" by Ellery Queen. I bought them both.

Despite my decade and a half search for an "old" Sherlock Holmes adventure, I've been very good at locating new stuff quickly. However, when I found a book that had been out for over a year without my knowledge, my loving and supportive wife made the statement, "You're slipping" to me. I was wounded. I considered myself a "book detective" having found copies of old or out-of-print books for many of my friends and dozens of lesser known Sherlock Holmes tomes for myself. One or two are bound to slip through the cracks now and again.

Unfortunately, her claim planted a seed of doubt in my mind. Could I actually be slipping in my eternal search for Sherlockian items to place in my collection? Were my powers fading? On one expedition to Chicagoland bookstores with a friend, I stated to him "there's one in here" as we crossed the threshold of the store. Within minutes I found a copy of "Sherlock Slept Here" about Sir Arthur Conan Doyle's visits to America, a book I did not have in my collection. My friend was amazed!

Was that intuition fading?

Was I ready for a beekeeping farm on the Sussex Downs much like my fabled hero?

I needed something to prove I wasn't becoming feeble when it came to finding Sherlockian collectibles.

So, when a Chicago radio personality friend of mine called to tell me there was an estate sale planned for a man from the north side of the city and he was a Sherlock Holmes fan, I made sure I had the ready cash and the day off to make the trip.

As fate would have it, my wife developed a cold the morning of the sale. I offered to stay home with her, but she insisted I go and see what I could add to the collection. I really enjoy "treasure hunting" with her and was a little disappointed I had to go alone, but I made sure she had plenty of chicken soup and orange juice and made the trip.

Upon arriving at the estate (and it was a pretty big house), I was informed the Sherlock Holmes collection had been donated to a local college.

Disappointing, to say the least.

I did find a small oak table and four chairs for our kitchen and made a small bid on that. My wife and I had been looking for just such an arrangement for a while and a fifty dollar bid didn't seem to be out of line.

What I didn't know was the lot also included an old Army trunk. When I won the bid, the table and chairs were loaded into the back of my truck along with the footlocker.

"What's this?" I asked the estate sale assistant.

"Dunno," he said looking at the invoice. "Comes with the table."

"Anything in it?" I asked.

He checked the invoice again.

"Linens. Napkins. Books," he said.

Books, I thought. I wonder...

I was never one to turn down a bargain and I knew my wife could find a way to make the trunk look like something you'd use as the center piece for a living room or office. She does a lot with crafts and crocheting.

I brought the items home and wrestled the table and chairs into the kitchen. My wife loved my choice and promised to get them looking like new as soon as she felt better.

"Why'd you buy that thing?" my wife asked upon seeing the Army trunk.

"It came with the kitchen set," I said. "It's supposed to have books in it."

"Not many if you were able to drag that thing in here alone," she said.

I agreed and got a hammer from my tool box under the kitchen sink.

"Do you want me to try to save this old lock?" I asked kneeling down in front of the chest.

"Looks pretty rusty," she said, and I took that to mean "No."

I hit the lock on its base and was immediately rewarded with it shattering open and sending a small dusting of rust onto the floor.

I removed the lock and opened the chest.

It appeared full of old, musty, yellowed linens and about a dozen napkins in the same condition.

"Can you do anything with these?" I asked.

"They're very delicate," my wife answered. "I don't know if they'll survive a good cleaning, but I'll try."

I removed the linens and napkins which seemed to fill the trunk, but at the bottom were four packed manila envelopes and a half dozen old books.

I assumed the envelopes were probably jammed with personal papers or something otherwise useless to me and removed them to examine the books.

The books were extremely old. The glue used on the bindings had dried and cracked. A couple of them had the beginning of mold growth. They were beyond repair and had to be disposed of in the trash.

What a bust, I thought, as I dragged the Army trunk out to the garage where it could air out without being exposed to the elements.

It wasn't until after dinner, when I was sure my wife was already feeling better, that I got to examine the manila envelopes.

I did it mostly out of curiosity, but I was stunned to discover something unexpected.

There were numbers written on the flaps of each envelope; one through four.

I opened the first envelope and discovered the name "Watson" written on a single sheet of paper. I immediately opened the other envelopes and discovered similar sheets of paper with different names on them. One was labeled "Mycroft" and the other two had "Gregson" and "Lestrade" written on them respectively.

As anyone reading this now will know, these names are easily recognizable to Sherlock Holmes fans. "Watson" is the faithful friend and companion of the great detective. "Mycroft" is Sherlock's older and smarter brother. "Gregson" and "Lestrade" are two of Scotland Yard's inspectors from the Holmes stories. Holmes described them as "the best of a bad lot," but I worked on a few police departments, and I can't believe they were as bad as he claimed.

This was the greatest Sherlockian find of my life! I definitely was NOT slipping.

I picked up the "Watson" file again and skimmed through it. It was a diary of sorts and it contained notes (some almost illegible) on a few of the cases yet to be recorded in the Holmes Canon.

The "Mycroft" file was the thinnest, but it also contained what appeared to be diary excerpts and government papers that mentioned Sherlock Holmes. The ones from the two detectives had typewritten police reports with hand-written addendum. The addendum all mentioned how Sherlock Holmes had been instrumental in solving the cases that were documented.

I'd spent three hours with these files before my wife pointed out how late it was getting and I had work in the morning. I'd have to wait to really go through the files.

So, on my next weekend, I used our recently purchased and refurbished kitchen table to organize the files into some kind of understandable order. I discovered they were detailed adventures of Sherlock Holmes and Dr. Watson with assistance from two of London's finest and the Great Detective's brother.

I have done my best to put these files into a coherent written text, but I am no Arthur Conan Doyle. The files are unprintable as they stand, but I have been able to piece together a series of unrelated adventures that involve principal characters from the Holmes stories. If you're reading this, please know I've done my best to preserve the original information, but writing from the twenty-first century will bring with it some inaccuracies in the style and tone of the original as well as the fact that some Americanisms are bound to be discovered by literary scholars.

I am a screenwriter by profession and this kind of narrative writing isn't my usual format. I have done my best to smooth out the stories. I discovered some facts that might contradict other facts written in the original sixty stories provided by Sir Arthur for his friend Dr. Watson. In the end, I feel the facts revealed here to be true and accurate to the best of my interpretation.

I leave the final determination to the reader.

Prologue

Dr. John H. Watson sat at the bedside of his wife, Mary, and held her delicate hand in his. Her pulse was weak and her breathing was shallow and labored. The pneumonia brought on by the influenza was destroying her. He would much rather have been attending to her at home, but she was so weak now, that only St. Bartholomew's Hospital would be able to properly administer to her.

Dr. Robinson entered and the grave expression on his face told Watson this was not going to be good news.

"You've done all you can," Watson said knowing the words Robinson would speak before Robinson had the opportunity to utter them himself. Watson had spoken those words many times in the past to families of some of his patients. They were difficult words to speak and with time never actually grew any easier. The least he could do for this good physician was say them before he had to. "But she's not improving."

"Her lungs are filling with fluid," Robinson added. "The time is short now."

Watson looked at Mary, and his heart swelled and broke simultaneously. He had "experience" with many women on three continents, but this was the only one he'd ever truly loved. His mother had died when he was a small child leaving only his father and older brother to raise him. Female affection was a rarity for him. After medical school he'd joined Her Majesty's Service and became an Army surgeon for the Fifth Northumberland Fusiliers where he was wounded in the leg at the Battle of Maiwand. It was a wound that caused discomfort at every change of the weather, but the pain of that injury was nothing like that of his broken heart.

Watson gazed at his wife and realized a courageous act was immediately called for; more courageous than any he'd ever had to perform in the past.

He had to let her go.

"I love you, Mary," Watson said whispering into his wife's ear and with a strength he didn't know he had. She didn't stir but somehow, Watson knew she could hear him. "You can go now. You don't need to hold on just for me. Just know that I love you and always will. I will see you again."

Mary took a deep but labored breath and let it out slowly. She did not take another.

Chapter One

Dr. John H. Watson, attired in his military uniform and accompanied by a couple of intimate acquaintances, followed the funeral procession through the immense and oddly silent Highgate Cemetery. There wasn't a great turnout for the funeral, and Watson felt a certain sense of depression for this. No one knew Mary Morstan the way he did. His love for her had been tremendous from the moment they'd met at the rooms he shared at 221B Baker Street and grown increasingly powerful over the few short years they'd had together.

Threatening clouds had formed over London in the early morning, making an already dreary day even drearier. No rain was yet falling, but the skies were promising a downpour at any moment.

The gray of the sky and the gray of the immense fields of grave markers provided almost no contrast leaving the expanse of heaven and earth a dreary, colorless morass.

"There are no children here," Watson thought as they passed numerous other grave sites. "I suppose that is something to be thankful for."

Watson and Mary had been married almost immediately after the adventure of the Sign of the Four **(1)** when Mary had come to Watson's friend, the great detective, Sherlock Holmes, for advice on what she believed to be a simple matter; whether or not to learn the truth of her father's disappearance.

Sherlock Holmes agreed to take the case and discovered a mystery that involved a secret stolen treasure, duplicitous military dealings and vengeful murder.

His marriage to Mary would take Watson away from his

familiar quarters at 221B Baker Street where he had shared rooms with Holmes. Mary had been there to comfort him after the tragic death of Sherlock Holmes during the final battle with his archnemesis, Professor James Moriarty at the Reichenbach Falls in Switzerland. Although he missed his friend and the life of near constant adventure, Watson loved the time he spent with Mary.

They'd tried for children, but the Lord never saw fit to bless them. It weighed heavy on Mary that she couldn't provide a child for her husband, but Watson constantly assured her their time together was more than enough happiness for him. However, he knew she desperately wanted a child for herself.

Tears began to fall from Watson's eyes as he followed the casket carrying his beloved wife.

"I've failed again," Watson said mainly to himself.

A reassuring arm was placed around his shoulders even as his sobs began to shake his body.

The arm belonged to Inspector Gerard Lestrade of Scotland Yard.

Lestrade was a short rodent-faced man who was much younger than he looked. He also had a very kind heart that allowed him to feel great compassion for the people near him. Holmes was never aware of the depth of admiration Lestrade had for him. It was Watson who was able to see Lestrade was more than just a regular client to Sherlock Holmes; he was a friend.

"We're here for you, Doctor," Lestrade said, but received no acknowledgment.

Watson continued his tearful march until they reached the grave-site. Then Watson straightened to military attention while the minister gave the benediction.

Watson didn't hear a single word.

The rain began to fall.

*   *   *

More than a week had passed since Mary's funeral. Dr. Watson had packed the house in Paddington and moved all of his belongings down and across the river to a house in Kensington where he'd also relocated his practice.

It had been a difficult task packing all of Mary's belongings; her dresses, her hair brushes, her knitting and sewing items, many of which Watson had no idea of their use. Everything she loved filled a half dozen boxes. All of it was donated to church organizations.

"They'll find usefulness somewhere," Watson thought as members of Mary's church offered their thanks and sympathy for his loss and carted away the boxes containing her life and his memories.

Watson kept a single photograph that he placed in his new examination room at his practice. It was aligned so only he would see it while sitting at his desk and consulting with a patient. In his pocket and attached to his keys was the pen knife she'd given him on their first anniversary. "To John with adoring love, Mary" was engraved on it. It had never been used in the years to follow, and Mary often asked why he carried it if he were never going to use it.

"Because you gave it to me," Watson told her time and again knowing she loved to hear that. "And I love you. I'd never risk damaging it."

There would still be some time of mourning for Watson. No rush to open the practice. His friend, Dr. Vernon was seeing to his patients in his absence. Vernon was a good man and made no complaints regarding the extra workload. In fact, he seemed oddly grateful for the additional consultations.

Watson looked around his new home and sighed.

This was not a happy place.

Without Mary, it never would be.

A loud knock at his front door snapped him out of his blue study, and there was momentary appreciation for the interruption.

"Who can be coming to me now?" Watson wondered as he crossed his living room to the main entrance.

Inspector Lestrade stood on his threshold.

Watson brightened slightly.

"Inspector," he said as cheerily as possible. "What do I owe the pleasure?"

"I'm...well..." Lestrade stuttered.

"Is everything all right?" Watson asked truly concerned.

Lestrade became suddenly serious.

"That's what I've come to ask you, Doctor," he said in an almost policeman-like tone. "Are YOU all right?"

Watson smiled weakly.

"Come in, Inspector," he said stepping aside so Lestrade could enter his new home.

Once inside, Lestrade looked around at the many unpacked and half-empty boxes. Furniture was scattered about the sitting room with no rhyme nor reason.

"I'm afraid I've had no time for decorating," Watson explained as he surveyed the clutter in his new home. "I'm also afraid I have no eye for decorating."

Lestrade and Watson shared a glance and both began to laugh softly.

"Thank you, Inspector," Watson said. "I've not laughed

in some time. I wish I could offer you something, tea or coffee, but the kitchen is as disorganized as every other room in this godforsaken place."

"You're not comfortable here?" Lestrade asked.

"Not in the least," Watson replied. "But it wouldn't matter where I was. Without Mary..."

"I know," Lestrade said gently and briefly placing an understanding arm around Watson's shoulders. "It's difficult losing someone so close to you. I've never known the love of a woman such as your Mary, but I recall how I felt when I lost my dear Mum. It's a wound that never quite heals, but..."

"But what?" Watson asked.

"But the pain will fade," Lestrade said knowingly. "I know you don't want to hear that now when you think it couldn't possibly, but it's true. The pain will fade."

Watson began to sob with the same fervor he had displayed at Mary's funeral. Lestrade guided Watson to a sofa where he cleared a number of files and boxes of other papers and helped Watson to a seat. Watson buried his face in his hands, racked by sobs of grief.

Lestrade pulled a chair from a grouping of chairs along a wall with two bow windows and placed it in front of the doctor.

"You can't let the grief win," Lestrade said taking a seat in front of Watson. "It will eat you alive. Mary wouldn't want this."

"I know," Watson agreed. "It's just...I can't...I feel..."

"What?" Lestrade asked. "What do you feel?"

Watson shook his head partly to clear it and partly because he simply did not know how to express the enormous depth to which his agony reached. It was like a bottomless pit with nothing to fill it, yet it continued to eat at him, devouring every tiny bit it could.

"You mentioned at the funeral something about failing again," Lestrade said. "What did you mean by that?"

Watson shook himself and drew in a deep cleansing breath.

"It was nothing," he answered.

"No. It was something."

"I'm not sure I wish to talk about it."

"Why not?"

"It's very painful, and I've embarrassed myself enough in front of you."

"You shouldn't feel embarrassed," Lestrade said reassuringly. "We are friends, you and I. If there's something I can do to help, I'm happy to do it."

Watson looked into Lestrade's face and didn't see the policeman he'd known for over a decade. He truly saw a friend.

"You're right," Watson said and resigned himself to tell Lestrade what he'd been feeling. "At the funeral, I felt as though I'd failed Mary. I couldn't make her well when the influenza came. I'm a doctor for Christ's sake, and I couldn't save the person most dear to me. All of my medical knowledge. All of the training I've had. I took her to London's best hospital. Nothing I did helped her and she died."

"Many people die of influenza every year," Lestrade said. "You can't blame yourself for that."

"But that wasn't the only thing," Watson began. "I failed Holmes too."

At this, Lestrade looked shaken.

"How can you say such a thing?" Lestrade asked. "He

was your friend; your best friend, from what I saw. You were with him at the end. That should have been a great honor."

Watson's eyes widened.

"But that's just it, Inspector," he said. "I wasn't with him. When we were in Switzerland, a boy had come to us with a plea from a sick Englishwoman. I knew this was a ruse. We'd been at the hotel and I'd not encountered any other Englanders. No one but Holmes and myself were from the Empire." **(2)**

"Then why did you fall for the ruse?"

"Because Holmes insisted," Watson said almost angrily. "I went back to the hotel at Holmes's insistence. I knew I should have stayed with him. I knew this boy was lying to us. He didn't even remain with me while I returned to the hotel. I should have just turned back around and rejoined my friend at the falls. Had I been there, maybe, together, we could have vanquished the evil Professor Moriarty and Holmes would still be alive."

"But you couldn't have known the outcome," Lestrade argued. "You couldn't have been certain anything would have changed. What if you had died? Mary would have been mourning you. Her last few years would have been spent alone."

Watson looked at Lestrade with a new-found admiration.

"Sherlock Holmes had many difficulties with you boys from the Yard," Watson said with a weak smile. "But he never, NEVER, clarified anything so succinctly as you just did at this moment. Thank you, Inspector."

Inspector Lestrade smiled genuinely.

"We do have our moments now and again, Dr. Watson," he said and a slight blush came to his cheeks. He was obviously not accustomed to receiving compliments. "What are your plans?"

"I gather you mean after unpacking?" Watson said.

"Yes," Lestrade answered looking again at the clutter. "I hadn't really thought about it. I've been postponing any other major decisions."

"Have you thought about continuing your writing with that other fellow?"

"Conan Doyle?"

"Yes," Lestrade said. "I hadn't given it much thought, actually."

"I think that might be good for you. Get your mind off...things."

"You might be right," Watson agreed. "I do have a number of undocumented cases involving Sherlock Holmes that might be worthy of public interest."

"How about that Baskerville one?" Lestrade asked. "I did pretty well in that one."

"I don't know," Watson said. "Holmes did very little in that one but bring you in and present the solution at the end."

"Between us," Lestrade said conspiratorially, "I think that's why I liked that one so much."

The two men laughed again.

Chapter Two

The weeks passed slowly for Dr. Watson, but gradually he was becoming aware the words of his friend, Inspector Lestrade, were true. The pain was fading. Minutely, but fading nonetheless. Still, his recent loss weighed heavy on him at times, and occasionally when he found himself not thinking of Mary, he felt guilt and shame for having let her slip his mind.

Gradually, more out of necessity than anything else, Dr. Watson began to live his life again. He had formed a routine with his daily activities and visits of his patients. His cooking skills were virtually non-existent and he had many of his meals out. He'd contemplated hiring a housekeeper to handle some limited cleaning and meal preparation, but he still felt apprehensive at having a woman in the house with him who was not his wife. The closeness of another female, even in a mere domestic capacity, was still out of the question.

It still wasn't easy in any case. His sleep was continually plagued by nightmares. He awoke in the darkness sure Mary had been calling him out of the darkness – only to discover he was still alone. At times it was maddening for him, but slowly, as his grief diminished and life returned, he knew the dreams would stop as well.

Dr. Watson took on additional medical responsibilities by volunteering as a police surgeon. He found his paths crossing occasionally with Inspectors Athelney Jones, Tobias Gregson and, most certainly, Gerard Lestrade.

Inspector Lestrade's work on the recent Molesley Mystery had been something of a sensation for the detective. Although, Watson's services as a surgeon weren't needed for a robbery case, he had accompanied Inspector Lestrade to the scene of the crime. A jewelry store in the West End had been burgled.

A fascinating method had been used to gain entry to the building. The lock on a fortified back door had been broken almost as if by the use of a small explosive device placed within the locking mechanism, but there had been no sound of an explosion and there was no evidence of flame or combustion. Upon examination, it appeared as if the lock had simply exploded of its own accord, but this was impossible. Such things never happen.

It was Inspector Lestrade who figured out the lock had been filled with water through the keyhole and then on a particularly cold evening had frozen and expanded rupturing the locking mechanism and allowing access to the jewelry store.

The burglars were quickly nabbed when they tried to sell the jewels to a fence who reported to the police. For all their wittiness in conceiving the crime, they were ultimately caught because of their simple greed.

Lestrade received a commendation from the Superintendent of Police, and his name was once again prominent in the London papers without the assistance of Sherlock Holmes. However, there had been an unflattering and uncalled for editorial in the Daily Telegraph touting the possibility that one of London's finest had something to do with the theft or else he would not have been able to solve the crime. Watson felt a small pang of guilt over this belief since his tales of mystery with Sherlock Holmes often portrayed the official detectives as "out of their element."

"How were you able to figure out the method the thieves

used?" Watson asked one evening after the crooks had been apprehended. He had invited Lestrade to a dinner out to celebrate his victory.

"I'd like to say I used the methods of our old friend," Lestrade answered as he sliced into a particularly delicious steak and kidney pie. "You know, when you have eliminated the impossible, and all that."

Watson chuckled.

"It was actually much easier," Lestrade continued. "When I was a boy, my father used a similar method to remove a rusted lock from an old gate. He waited for a particularly frigid evening, poured water into the lock and checked back the next day. The lock had popped and the gate could be opened."

"Amazing!" Watson said. "But that's exactly how Holmes would have done it."

Stunned, the inspector asked, "But how?"

"Holmes used all of his knowledge to solve crimes. You did the same. Holmes believed the more information someone knew, the more they could figure out different circumstances. He often claimed there was nothing new under the sun which was why he kept clippings of crimes from all over the world. He believed somewhere someone had attempted the same type of crime and knowing how it was committed could lead to who had committed it."

"Aren't you talking about the same fellow who didn't know that the Earth revolved around the sun?"

"I am."

"Then how can you compare the two of us that way?"

"Simple," Watson said. "You and Holmes used knowledge you'd both gained to solve a mystery. Holmes used to say he tried to fill his 'brain attic' with all the relevant information he would need to be a successful consulting detective. He didn't want any unnecessary clutter to his encyclopedic mind, so facts like the orbit of the Earth were irrelevant to him."

"So was how my old man dismantled a rusty lock until I needed it to solve a crime," Lestrade countered. "So who's to say what information is important and what isn't?"

"You're absolutely right, Inspector," Watson agreed. "Who is to say? Perhaps Holmes was wrong. Perhaps all knowledge can be useful in one matter or another. All I know is, Holmes wanted his mind clear of information he believed he'd never use when it came to crime solving. I think he was simply 'hedging his bets' when he chose what he studied and this way appeared quite brilliant because he was an expert in so many fields."

"His was a unique intellect," Lestrade said. "I will give him that."

The two men finished their meal with further reminiscences of their friend, Sherlock Holmes.

*   *   *

"Feels a little blustery tonight," Watson said once the two men had finished dinner and paid the bill and were standing on the sidewalk outside of the restaurant. "It's like this March doesn't want to end and allow springtime."

"Indeed," Lestrade said turning up the collar of his coat. "Thank you for the dinner, Doctor. It was most delicious."

"You are very welcome, Inspector, and you deserved it," Watson said. "A remarkable job, once again."

"Thank you," Inspector Lestrade said again. "Do you

wish to share a cab home?"

"I think I'll walk, if that's all right. I want to do a little thinking, and the brisk night air will help."

"Well, I'm going to get out of this wind."

Inspector Lestrade raised his arm to a passing cab which swerved violently to reach the curb.

The Inspector gave his address to the driver as he was stepping into the four-wheeler.

"Take care, Doctor," Lestrade said as the cab began to move.

"You too, Inspector," Watson said as he watched the cab drive off.

Watson stuck his hands into his pockets and began to walk along the sidewalk in the general direction of his new home. He had a short trek of perhaps six blocks. His mind immediately turned to memories of his great friend.

"Does grief turn our memories against us?" Watson wondered as he walked. "Was I tearing down Holmes's reputation while praising Lestrade for his accomplishment?"

This thought troubled the doctor and he contemplated it all the way to the front door of his new home.

How he dreaded going through that door into the silence beyond. No one was home. No one ever would be. Desolation. Loneliness. Silence. That's what awaited him beyond his front door. If only spring would come and provide the hope of new life.

"It's better than standing out in the wind," Watson mumbled to himself and removed his key from his pocket and opened the door.

Inside, Watson built a fire in the hearth and dragged his

armchair closer to the blaze. Further unpacking would wait until the morning. Tonight he had a decision to make. Was he going to wallow in further misery at all he had lost so far in his life, or was he going to do whatever needed doing to get out of this dark study and back into the world of the living?

It would be a long night.

Chapter Three

The morning following the celebration dinner Watson shared with Inspector Lestrade, began as most days for most London household employees. There was silver to polish, dusting to do, and shopping to complete. The latter was Lydia Caine's favorite task and she was allowed to perform it because she was also the cook at Lord Fairchild's home. Lydia was a slight girl with soft blond curls that framed her face and brought out the deep blue of her eyes. She'd hated the curls since childhood but they did well to accentuate her delicate facial features and elevate her to something of a beauty rather than being simply attractive.

Lydia insisted on doing the shopping because the original cook hated doing it and would usually send a houseboy to run the errands. More often than not, the houseboy would find an outside interest that would waylay his accomplishing the task in a timely fashion. This would result in the boy either coming home with whatever remnants were left of the day's offerings at market or, had he completed the shopping before his extracurricular activities, their freshness would be greatly diminished. Lydia performed the task with precision and economy often obtaining fresh cuts of meat and recently harvested vegetables for below asking price.

It wasn't long before Lord Fairchild decided to let the original cook go and allow Lydia to immediately step into the position. It was on a voluntary basis at first. However, her culinary talents were well-received, and she soon found herself a permanent fixture as the household cook.

Lydia did that day's shopping and upon her return began

the cooking.

She was alone in the Fairchild house as this was the day set aside for most of the staff to have the day off.

Lord Fairchild, a strong, good-looking man of nearly thirty years with thick brown hair and a professional air about him despite his "man of action" appearance, was at work at the bank where he was a finance manager.

Lady Fairchild, a dainty woman of just over twenty-four years and blessed with an inner strength that remained hidden unless challenged, had their six month old son at her mother's house for a visit.

Lydia insisted the Fairchild family have healthy, delicious meals every day; not just days when the servants were present. She worked without a day off. She believed if you loved what you did, you never actually worked and Lydia loved the Fairchilds as if they were her own family. She never truly felt like an employee with them. Everything she did was to make life better for her employers.

Lydia's dedication was not lost on the Fairchilds. Lord Fairchild paid Lydia well, and she was allowed to keep any overages from the shopping money which was an extravagance for Lydia. She was very frugal but not cheap. The pride she took in her cooking made her indispensable to the Fairchilds. They often showed off her talents by having dinner parties for friends and many of Lord Fairchild's work companions. It was even rumored a recent promotion was due in part to the culinary expertise of Lydia that had swayed the judgment of Lord Fairchild's supervisors.

Most of Lydia's culinary education came from research she did at London's libraries.

"Anything you might ever want to learn is free," Lydia's father once told her. "Just check at the libraries or the museums. You can learn about anything at those places." So, Lydia learned about cooking and just as a sculptor can see a statue in a block of marble or a painter can see a picture on a blank canvas or a writer can see an entire book on an empty sheet of paper, Lydia could see and taste meals in her mind even if she'd never prepared them or eaten them in the past.

She was an artist with food and her mind was an encyclopedia of recipes and substitutions she could employ in meal preparation.

On one occasion, Lydia was tasked with preparing a special dinner for Lord Fairchild when he had invited a special envoy from Italy to dinner.

Lydia worked hard to find the perfect menu and was able to produce an authentic Italian meal.

"This is absolutely delicioso!" the envoy declared.

The Fairchilds were extremely pleased with Lydia's dinner and the impression it left on the Italian envoy.

"I feel I have been transported back to my homeland," he said as he finished his dessert of baked honey clusters. "Please to let me meet the man so capable of recreating my favorite foods."

The Fairchilds were overwhelmed by the exuberance shown by their guest and had no choice but to honor his request.

Lady Fairchild excused herself from the dining room table and went to the kitchen to speak with Lydia.

"Lydia," Lady Fairchild said, spying her young cook as she tidied up the ingredients from the evening's meal.

"Yes, Lady Fairchild?" Lydia said with a short curtsey as

she wiped her hands on her apron.

"Our guest would like to speak with you," Lady Fairchild said attempting to hide a smile.

Suddenly worried, Lydia replied, "Is he displeased? I tried my best. I fear I may have heated the honey a little too long for the dessert. I hope –"

"Please, Lydia, just come with me," Lady Fairchild said firmly leading the way out of the kitchen.

Nervously, Lydia followed the woman to the dining room where the guest and Lord Fairchild remained at the table now sharing cigars and brandy.

"Senor DiGilio," Lord Fairchild said standing. "I'd like to present our cook, Lydia Caine."

Lydia curtsied again and bowed her head.

"I apologize if the dinner was not to your liking, sir," Lydia said nearly on the verge of tears. "It was my first time preparing such a meal. I promise I will do better in the future if you should visit again."

Senor DiGilio stood and walked over to Lydia.

"Senora," he said. "Please. You have nothing to apologize for. You are a genius. If I thought for a moment I could, I would whisk you away to Italia with me to be MY cook."

At this, Senor DiGilio laughed as did Lord and Lady Fairchild although both harbored a secret concern Lydia would go with him.

"I'm afraid we couldn't allow that," Lord Fairchild immediately stated. "Lydia is a firm fixture in the Fairchild household, and she always will be."

Now, tears did fall from Lydia's eyes, but they were tears of joy and relief. She loved working in the Fairchild home but she never once thought for even a moment that they were as fond of her as she was of them. She was instantly eased at discovering they were.

Lydia's dinners became famous throughout London to the point where Lord Fairchild was often besieged with requests to host dinner parties for banking officials, and Lady Fairchild would be requested to handle the meals for the clubs and associations to which she belonged. Lydia had occasionally been invited to teach cooking at local restaurants and offered head chef positions despite her gender, but she always turned them down. Her loyalty was solely to the Fairchilds, and it would remain thus.

This wasn't to say she hit the mark every time with her meals. There were occasional missteps, but nothing so serious as to cause anything more than the recipe's removal from Lydia's mental collection and a laugh or two from the Fairchilds.

On this Monday Lydia was making one of her simpler dishes, but one the Fairchilds especially enjoyed; a beef stew from the American West. It was done with vegetables, thick beef cuts and a gravy enhanced with garlic and flour to thicken the mix. She sided it with slices of her fresh baked bread and sweet butter. Lord Fairchild would pair it with a dark red wine from his personal cellar.

Lydia was busily chopping the vegetables when the intruder entered.

Silently, he stole up behind her, then swiftly placed his gloved left hand over her mouth while grasping her right wrist with his gloved right hand. He forced the knife from her hand and she dropped it on the cutting board in front of her.

"Don't scream," the intruder whispered. "Do you understand me?"

Lydia nodded shaking with fear.

Why was this happening? She wondered, terrified. Was this real?

Slowly the intruder took his had away from her mouth.

"If you make a noise, you'll die," he said. "If you turn around, you'll die."

"What do you want?" Lydia asked in a terrified whisper following the instructions not to turn around.

"I need your help with something," the intruder said.

"Help? With what?"

"I just need you to stare straight ahead and don't move."

"Are you robbing the house?" Lydia asked.

"No," the intruder said chuckling.

The intruder's laugh caused an involuntary shudder to pass through Lydia's body.

"I said, don't move," the intruder restated the moment he detected her shiver, all humor gone from his tone. "If you move, you die. If you scream, you die. If you reach for that knife while I'm here with you, you die. Understand?"

Lydia nodded again.

Lydia was still standing rigid as a tent pole at the kitchen counter when Lady Fairchild returned home with her baby some thirty or so minutes later.

"Lydia?" Lady Fairchild said upon discovering her cook frozen with fear at the kitchen counter. "Are you all right?"

"Is he gone?" Lydia whispered.

"Who?"

"The man. Is he gone?"

Lady Fairchild, still carrying her infant son, walked up to Lydia and for the first time saw the panic and fear on her face and the perspiration she was drenched in.

"Dear Lord," Lady Fairchild whispered. "What has happened to you?"

Still too frightened to move, Lydia said, "A man came in. He threatened me if I moved. He said he'd kill me."

"Let's go," Lady Fairchild said clutching her son to her breast and grabbing Lydia with her other hand.

"No," Lydia said paralyzed with terror. "He'll kill us."

"Lydia," Lady Fairchild said. "I think he's gone, but to be safe we have to leave the house. We have to get a policeman."

Finally, Lydia moved her head and looked at Lady Fairchild. Lydia nodded and Lady Fairchild guided her, at first slowly then at a quickened pace through the kitchen and through the living area and finally out onto the street.

Lady Fairchild hollered for help to an elderly neighbor gentleman who happened to be leaving his front door the moment Lady Fairchild and Lydia were leaving their home across the street. He approached Lady Fairchild thinking something was wrong with the baby who had begun to wail.

"What's wrong, mum?" the elderly neighbor inquired and then noticed Lady Fairchild was carrying her baby. "Is it the babe?"

"No," Lady Fairchild said. "We're fine. Someone broke into our house."

Lady Fairchild described the situation and was ushered into the neighbor's house while he hurriedly went in search of the constable who patrolled their block.

It was only a few moments, but it seemed like an eternity before the gentleman returned with a young police officer in tow. He had a physically fit physique and hazel green eyes that burned with dedication for his duties.

"What's happened, ma'am?" the officer asked.

Lady Fairchild provided the officer with her address across the street and gave yet another short description of what she'd encountered in her home.

"Can these people stay here for a few minutes?" the officer asked the gentleman.

"Of course," he replied.

"I'll be right back," the officer said and immediately left the neighbor's house.

Lydia and Lady Fairchild heard three short blasts from the constable's whistle and a moment later three more. Less than a minute after that, another officer much shorter than the first and a few years older and a police sergeant who bore a thick mustache and a pot belly were outside and crossing the street. They entered the house each with his truncheon drawn.

Another eternity passed before the three officers of the law exited the house. The sergeant spoke briefly to the second Bobby who sprinted down the street and out of sight. Together the sergeant and the constable dispersed a small crowd that had gathered in the street in front of the Fairchild Home.

Lydia and Lady Fairchild were brought outside the neighbor's house to the sidewalk.

"Checked the whole house, ma'am," the young officer said once he'd crossed the street. "No one's in there now."

"Thank heavens for that," Lady Fairchild said relieved. "Where is that other officer going in such a hurry?"

"He's off to request an inspector, ma'am," the young officer stated and waved the sergeant to join him.

"An inspector? Surely, that isn't necessary."

"We don't know, ma'am. Mighty strange occurrence, this."

At that moment the sergeant joined them on the sidewalk in front of the neighbor's home.

"Sergeant John Rance, ma'am," the sergeant introduced himself taking off his helmet. "And this is Constable Evert."

"Ma'am," the constable said tipping his helmet toward Lady Fairchild and then again toward Lydia to whom he smiled warmly. Lydia looked away partially out of shyness but also because she still hadn't gotten over the fright the intruder caused her.

"This constable tells me you're having an inspector come around," Lady Fairchild said.

"Yes, Ma'am," the sergeant said replacing his helmet. "This is a very odd thing. Very odd. Just want to dot all my i's and cross all my t's if you don't mind. Always good to have a superior officer double-check things. Just in case something was overlooked."

"I suppose I understand," Lady Fairchild claimed but didn't really comprehend the reasoning.

"If you feel up to it, I'd like you to look through the house before he arrives and make sure nothing's been stolen," Sergeant Rance said.

"You're staying with us, aren't you, sergeant?" Lady Fairchild asked.

"Yes, Ma'am. I'll wait. As will Constable Evert."

They all crossed the street together then the two police officers followed Lady Fairchild and Lydia into the home.

"I'm going to put my child down for his nap," Lady Fairchild said of the sleeping babe in her arms.

"If you want, I'll accompany you, ma'am," Sergeant Rance offered.

"No," she said. "I'll be only a moment."

True to her word, Lady Fairchild was back in a few seconds.

"Where shall we begin?" she asked.

"Anywhere you'd like," the sergeant answered.

Lady Fairchild began to walk the downstairs rooms while Lydia and Constable Evert took seats in the drawing room.

"Scary, hmm?" Evert said when he was alone with Lydia. He removed his constable's helmet and placed it on a thin, short table between the two chairs they were occupying in the sitting room. He had wavy, light brown hair, but some of that might have been caused by wearing the helmet.

"You don't know," Lydia said in a hushed voice and a slight shudder ran through her. "I've never been so terrified in all my life. Never."

"You're all right, though," he said comfortingly.

Lydia looked into the constable's eyes and he finally saw the fear she was feeling.

"I don't know if I am," she said. "I don't want to be alone in the house."

"You're not alone," he said.

"But I will be," she whispered trying to hide her concerns from Lady Fairchild. "They trust me here. They know I can handle the household and I'm capable of running the house alone. They will leave me again. What'll I do then?"

Lydia's voice was growing louder with fright. She had to stop speaking to keep quiet.

"We'll find the man who scared you," Evert said. "He

won't be able to do it again."

"I don't even know what he looks like," Lydia said angrily, partially at the intruder who'd terrorized her and partially at herself for not being brave enough to fight. "I was too scared to turn and look. He threatened to kill me if I did."

"Then you did the right thing," Evert said compassionately. "You don't want to jeopardize your own safety."

"But how can you catch someone I never even saw?"

"Do you think you could recognize his voice?"

"He spoke in a whisper."

"Still, there might be a clue there," Evert assured.

"I just don't know," Lydia placed her hands over her face and sobbed.

Evert patted her gently on the knee.

"It'll be fine," he said reassuringly although his tone was less certain. She was probably correct in assuming the intruder would never be apprehended; at least, not for this crime.

A moment later Sergeant Rance and Lady Fairchild returned and joined Lydia and Evert in the drawing room.

"Is anything missing?" Lydia asked when she spied Lady Fairchild.

"Nothing I can see," Lady Fairchild stated, a bit relieved. "But we'll have Mr. Fairchild go through his things to determine if he's missing anything."

"So, it's not a burglary?" Evert asked Rance.

"Doesn't appear to be," Rance replied.

"Then what happened here?" Evert asked puzzled.

"Hard to say," Rance answered. "We're going to have to wait for the inspector to arrive and let him take the lead on this.

Mighty strange indeed, I say."

Rance pulled his pocket watch out of his vest pocket and glanced at the time.

"How long ago did I send for the inspector?" Rance asked Evert.

"Seems to me about twenty minutes, maybe a bit longer."

"That's what I thought. I wonder what's keeping him."

"Want me to have a check?" Evert offered.

"Yes, good idea."

"Won't you please stay?" Lydia pleaded reaching out and taking hold of Evert's wrist and looking into his eyes. "I'd feel so much better if you were to stay here."

"I'll be staying behind, ma'am," Rance said with a faint smile. "Gotta brief the inspector when he arrives anyway."

"I'd feel better if it was you," Lydia said never taking her gaze from Constable Evert.

Lady Fairchild and Sgt. Rance shared an amused glance despite the seriousness of the situation.

"Sergeant?" Evert asked looking at Rance for guidance.

"Stay here, Evert," Rance said resignedly. "I'll be back in a tick."

Lydia was instantly more at ease.

"I'll show you out, sergeant," Lady Fairchild said and guided the policeman out of the drawing room.

Outside the front door, Sgt. Rance took a moment to speak with Lady Fairchild.

"Are you certain something happened here today?" Rance asked in a hushed tone.

"What do you mean?" Lady Fairchild asked.

"It doesn't seem odd that your only employee on the

premises today would have such an encounter?"

"I'm still lost, Sergeant."

"Has she ever experienced anything like this in the past?"

"No."

"Are you sure?"

"She's never said anything."

"Is she happy working here? Her wages? Working conditions? Fellow employees?"

"She's very happy," Lady Fairchild said. "She's been offered other positions but has always turned them down to remain in our employ. My husband and I are pleased to have her with us, and she's compensated quite well."

"I see."

"I don't think you do," Lady Fairchild countered. "She is not prone to flights of fancy or an overactive imagination. If my Lydia claims someone entered the house and threatened her, then, Sergeant Rance, that is exactly what happened."

"My apologies, ma'am," Rance said. "I meant no offense. I am merely trying to make sense of this situation."

"I understand," Lady Fairchild said and appeared to soften quite a bit. "Everyone is suspicious to a policeman."

Sgt. Rance smiled.

"In some ways that's correct, ma'am," he said. "Well, I'll be off to the Yard to find an inspector."

With that, Sgt. Rance left the front door of the Fairchild house and made his way down the street.

Lady Fairchild watched him retreat into the distance and stop to speak to a well-dressed gentleman with a walking stick, a military gate and a mustache who had just rounded the corner. The two men spoke for a few moments, and it appeared they were acquainted with one another. Finally, Sgt. Rance shook the man's hand then pointed at the Fairchild home and the man continued walking toward Lady Fairchild.

Perhaps this is the inspector, Lady Fairchild thought as she watched the gentleman approach.

"Lady Fairchild?" the gentleman asked from the sidewalk upon his arrival.

"Yes," she said. "May I help you?"

"My name is Dr. John Watson," the gentleman said and there was a stirring in Lady Fairchild's memory upon the mention of the name. "I was instructed by Inspector Lestrade to meet him here."

"Inspector Lestrade?" she asked. "I've not heard of him, but your name sounds familiar."

Dr. Watson smiled which caused an amusing rumpling of his distinguished mustache

"I used to work with the detective Sherlock Holmes," he said. "Now, I occasionally assist the police on criminal matters."

"Oh," Lady Fairchild said with dawning recognition. "I've seen your name in the paper quite often mentioned with Mr. Holmes. And I think there was a book...A Study in...Something?"

"Scarlet," Watson said. "A Study in Scarlet." **(3)**

"Yes, that's it. My husband read it. Not quite for me, I'm afraid."

"Perfectly understandable, Lady Fairchild," Watson agreed knowing that the bloody murder scene from the first adventure he'd shared with his great friend would not be something in line with the tastes of such a lady. However, he'd been surprised in the past at the interests of women. His own

Mary was a fan of Edgar Allen Poe.

"It was good seeing Sergeant Rance again," Watson said pointing his walking stick down the street in the direction from which he'd come. "He was only an officer when I first met him in the case mentioned in that book your husband read."

"What a small world," Lady Fairchild said.

"Indeed," Watson said. "It's good to see he's moved up a bit in the ranks."

"He was very capable while he was here," Lady Fairchild explained.

"That is good to hear," Watson said, his smile beginning to fade. "Well, I don't wish to keep you, Lady Fairchild. I'm happy to wait out here for Inspector Lestrade."

"Nonsense," she countered. "You'll come and have some tea and wait inside."

Lady Fairchild turned around with a rustling of her skirts and entered the house beckoning for Dr. Watson to follow.

Inside, Watson was shown to the drawing room and introduced to Lydia and Constable Evert who were advised of the reason for his visit.

"Dr. Watson needs no introduction to me," Evert said standing and shaking the good doctor's hand. "I've read his work and followed his adventures with Sherlock Holmes in the newspapers and on official police reports. It's an honor, sir."

"You're very kind," Watson said shaking the young constable's hand. "Now, can someone fill me in on what's happened here to cause this household such worry?"

Dr. Watson glanced at Lydia who clearly still appeared somewhat panic stricken.

Constable Evert briefed Dr. Watson on the facts of the

intrusion, sparse as they were.

"You're certain you're all right, my dear," Watson said in a comforting voice to Lydia.

"I'm not harmed," Lydia said. "Not physically, but my nerves, Doctor. I was so scared. I've never felt that frightened in my whole life."

"I can give you a mild sedative, if you'd like," Watson offered looking to Lady Fairchild.

"I think that might be within reason, considering the circumstances," Lady Fairchild agreed.

"But for later," Constable Evert stated. "I'm sure the inspector is going to want to speak with the young lady, and he'll want her alert and attentive."

"Certainly," Dr. Watson said. "I'll leave a sleeping draft which should give you some rest later this evening."

Lydia nodded.

There was a slight commotion at the front door and a moment later, Lord Fairchild entered the drawing room; a look of surprise and concern on his face at the sight of Lydia in distress and a uniformed policeman in his home.

"What's happened here?" Lord Fairchild asked and suddenly grew anxious. "Our son. Is he all right?"

"He's fine, darling. He was with me all afternoon. Come with me," Lady Fairchild said and guided her husband from the room.

In the hallway outside the drawing room, Lady Fairchild detailed the incident of the intruder and the adverse effect it had had on Lydia.

"How could this happen?" he asked. "This is one of the safest areas of London. I would never put my family or any of my employees in harm's way."

"I know, darling," Lady Fairchild said. "You are a wonderful provider."

"Then how did he get in? What did he want?"

"From what I've been told, he may have entered through the front door. Lydia had just returned with the grocery shopping. She may have simply forgotten to lock the door upon her arrival."

"A crime of opportunity?" Lord Fairchild asked. "Was anything taken?"

"Not that I could tell, but the police sergeant said you should look through your belongings and personal effects and see if anything is missing."

"Is that the officer in the drawing room?"

"No, that's Constable Evert."

"The other man, then?"

"No, believe it or not, that's Dr. Watson from that Sherlock Holmes story you so enjoyed."

"Dr. Watson?" Lord Fairchild was stunned that such a personage would be at his home. "What brings him here?"

"He says he was summoned by Inspector Lestrade," Lady Fairchild explained.

"I'm getting confused," Lord Fairchild said scratching his head. "There has been a police sergeant AND a police inspector here?"

"No, just the sergeant. The inspector is supposed to be on his way."

"But before he arrived, he sent a message summoning Dr. Watson?"

"Yes, that's right."

"Why isn't he here yet?"

"We don't know. The police sergeant went to inquire."

Lord Fairchild nodded.

"Lydia," he said. "She wasn't harmed?"

"No, but she's horribly frightened," Lady Fairchild said.

"I can imagine," Lord Fairchild agreed. "Well, I'd best check through my home office and my belongings to see if I'm missing anything of value."

Lady Fairchild agreed.

"I'm preparing some tea but I'll sit with Lydia and our other guests and wait for you," she said. "Do come back to the drawing room once you've finished."

"All right, dear," Lord Fairchild said. "You're taking this remarkably well. How are you staying so strong?"

"Something I learned from a wonderful man," Lady Fairchild said and smiled.

"Your father?" Lord Fairchild asked.

"No," Lady Fairchild said taking her husband's hand. "You."

Lord Fairchild pulled his wife to him and kissed her on the forehead.

"My darling," he said. "You're a wonderful woman."

Lord Fairchild released her to return to the drawing room then walked upstairs to make an inventory of his belongings.

"Quietly," she instructed her husband. "Timothy is down for his nap."

"Yes, dear," Lord Fairchild acquiesced.

Lady Fairchild went to the kitchen to fetch the tea then returned to the drawing room.

"How are you, my dear," she asked of Lydia as she filled the cups with tea from the tea pot.

45

"I don't know, ma'am," Lydia said refusing the offer of tea. "I'm so sorry to have caused this trouble."

"It's not your fault, Lydia," Lady Fairchild countered.

"Not at all," Dr. Watson said accepting his cup.

"No, indeed," Evert insisted also denying the offer of tea.

"I just wish I could help more," Lydia said despondently. "If only I could remember something about the man. If only I'd seen him."

"If you had," Evert said as Lord Fairchild returned to the sitting room. "There'd be a good chance things would have turned out for the worse."

Dr. Watson sent a stern look at Constable Evert who'd realized too late this was probably not the right thing to say even if it were true. Lord Fairchild had entered the drawing room at the exact same moment.

Lydia burst into a series of sobs, and Lady Fairchild had to escort her from the room.

"Well done," Lord Fairchild said to Constable Evert.

"I knew it was wrong to say the moment I said it," Evert remarked.

"Well, in the future," Lord Fairchild said. "You'll know better."

"I will, sir," Evert said. "My apologies."

"What is keeping this inspector of yours?" Fairchild asked.

"I'm sure I don't know, sir," Evert said. "I'll take my leave and wait for him outside."

However, Evert did not have to wait. The front bell rang almost simultaneously with his statement.

"I'll be back in a moment," Fairchild said moving toward

the drawing room door.

"Wait a moment, sir," Evert said. "It might be the intruder again. We really don't know who's at the door. I'd better accompany you."

"I'm perfectly capable of answering my own door, Constable. Besides, why would the intruder return and ring the bell first announcing to everyone inside that he'd arrived?"

Lord Fairchild then left to answer the door leaving Dr. Watson and Constable Evert alone in the drawing room.

"I..." Evert said running a hand through his hair, "am an idiot."

"Don't be too hard on yourself, young man," Watson said in a comforting tone. "You're bound to make mistakes now and again. Even my old friend made them on occasion."

"I just feel as though I've made matters worse for Lydia," Evert said.

"You may well have," Watson said. "Now you have to set things right. It's not difficult to tell that girl feels an attraction to you. You can't let her down."

"I'm not here looking for any kind of romantic entanglement, Doctor."

"That may be true, but she sees things differently."

"How so?"

"She asked that you remain while Sergeant Rance went back to the Yard. That tells you nothing?"

"I thought it was because we were closer in age; that she saw me as a kind of peer or something."

Watson chuckled.

"You do have a lot to learn, Evert," Watson said.

Before Evert could say anything else, Lord Fairchild

returned but not with Inspector Lestrade as was expected. The man accompanying Lord Fairchild was a tall, somewhat pale, flaxen-haired man with a slightly oversized notebook sticking out of his jacket pocket.

"Tobias Gregson," Watson said elated. **(4)** "Good to see you again, Inspector."

"So you know each other?" Fairchild asked.

"Of course," Watson said. "We've worked together in the past."

"The last time was...uh...'The Greek Interpreter,' wasn't it Doctor?" Gregson asked.

"Yes," Watson said, "among others."

"Perhaps we could save this reunion for another time?" Fairchild said more as a sarcastic statement than a request. He was obviously eager to have this matter settled and see a return to normal life for his household.

"That's true," Gregson agreed removing his notebook from his pocket. "Constable, will you inform me of the facts regarding this incident?"

Evert recounted the entire afternoon for Inspector Gregson who made numerous notes in his book as the story was told to him.

"You're absolutely certain nothing was taken?" Gregson asked Fairchild.

"Yes, Inspector," Fairchild answered. "My wife and I have been through the whole house. If something is missing, it's something of little or no value."

"Hmm," Gregson muttered. "That is odd."

"What plans do you have for this case?" Fairchild asked.

"For now, we'll post an officer in front and back to keep

a watch on the house," Gregson explained. "In case the intruder returns."

"I'd like to volunteer for the first watch, sir," Evert interjected.

"So it will be," Gregson said. "Meanwhile, we'll follow a couple of avenues the Yard has at its disposal and see what turns up."

"See what turns up," Fairchild said unimpressed. "I see."

"It's a strange matter, Lord Fairchild," Gregson said. "You must admit that yourself."

Fairchild stared directly at Gregson for an uncomfortable moment then softened.

"It is," Fairchild conceded. "I am at a loss for a motive if theft is ruled out."

"You see our problem, then," Gregson said.

"I suppose I do."

"Now," Gregson said turning to Dr. Watson and Constable Evert. "I'd like to speak with you two gentlemen outside."

"I'll show you out," Fairchild offered and led the way to the front door.

"I'll be right out here if you need anything, Lord Fairchild," Evert said brightly after the trio had exited the house.

"I feel safer already," Fairchild said with a distinct tone of sarcasm. "In any case, I think I'll clean and load my old service revolver."

With that, Lord Fairchild retreated into his home shutting the door with more of a slam than a gentle click.

"I'm not gaining any ground with him," Evert said to Dr. Watson.

"Why would you need to?" Gregson asked.

"There seems to be an attraction by the young lady, the victim of the intrusion, to young Constable Evert here," Watson explained with a smile.

"Is that so?" Gregson asked smiling as well.

"And, if I'm not mistaken, I think the attraction goes both ways?" Watson said.

Evert's cheeks reddened.

"She is a dainty thing," Evert said.

"She is indeed," Watson agreed.

"I just hope I haven't ruined things," Evert said, the redness dissipating.

"Why?" Gregson asked. "What happened?"

"He was a bit...indelicate with an explanation a few minutes before you arrived," Watson explained.

Gregson laughed softly.

"They are a different breed, the ladies," Gregson said.

"But why are you here, Inspector?" Watson asked. "I received a telegram from Lestrade stating I was to meet him here to assist in looking into this matter."

"You were?" Gregson asked. "I was not advised. I was told you'd recently moved to this area. I just assumed you were acquainted with the Fairchilds."

"Being new to the area," Watson said. "I'm not really acquainted with any of my neighbors who aren't already my patients."

"Hmm. And Rance didn't come back with news?" Gregson asked.

"News of what, Inspector?" Evert asked.

"Then you truly aren't aware?" Gregson asked. "You

haven't been told?"

"Told what?" Watson asked.

"That Inspector Lestrade has disappeared," Gregson said.

Chapter Four

When Sgt. Rance left the Fairchild home, he was slightly upset with being overruled by a subordinate officer simply because a housemaid was enamored with him. However, maintaining peace in an already disrupted household seemed a better avenue and gave him the opportunity to think as he walked. He enjoyed walking his beat. It gave him the chance to observe his surroundings and be ever vigilant for anything out of the ordinary.

By the time he'd reached the end of the block, his spirits had lifted and he was in for a great surprise. Around the corner came one of the two men who had given him the opportunity to look at his life differently and make a change for the better. Sgt. Rance knew there was no way for him to meet the first, but he also never truly expected to encounter the second.

Dr. John Watson, famous for tellings of the Sherlock Holmes adventures, had just rounded the corner.

"My goodness," Rance said upon reaching Dr. Watson. "You are Dr. Watson from the Sherlock Holmes stories."

"I am," Watson said but quickly added, "but I'm afraid my services are needed elsewhere at the moment, Officer. I wish I could speak with you, but—"

"I'm John Rance," he interrupted. "We met in the Lauriston Gardens case." **(5)**

Watson took a moment to look closer at the police sergeant and slowly recognized the man from nearly a decade and a half earlier; an officer Holmes claimed would "never rise in the force" because he'd let the killer of Enoch Drebber escape from the scene after being taken in by a simple ruse.

"You're a sergeant now," Watson said, observing the rank insignia on Rance's lapel and showing only slight surprise given Holmes's initial judgment of the man.

"Yes," Rance said proudly. "And I owe that to you, sir."

"Me?" Watson asked surprised again.

"Well, to be honest, Sherlock Holmes and you. I have read and re-read your stories with Mr. Holmes over and over. You might say I've been a-studying them. Mr. Holmes and his methods have been an inspiration to me, sir. I've improved myself greatly."

"Well," Watson said growing slightly impatient but still eager to hear this man's tale. "That's wonderful, Rance."

"I wish I could thank Mr. Holmes himself," Rance continued but a little sadly. "I was sorry to hear of his passing, sir. If he hadn't said to me 'Rance, that head of yours should be for use and not just ornament" I would probably still be a regular patrolman. Thank you, Dr. Watson, and bless you. You have changed my life. Anything I can ever do for you, you just ask. Hear?"

"Thank you, SERGEANT Rance," Watson said and offered his hand. "It's good to hear of your obvious and well-deserved success and my small assistance in it."

Rance shook Watson's hand vigorously.

"I have to be going," Watson said. "I'm supposed to meet Inspector Lestrade at the Fairchild house on this block."

"I was just on my way to fetch the Inspector," Rance said. "The Fairchild house is just down the street a piece. You can see Lady Fairchild still standing at her front door."

"That's the house, then?"

"Yes, Doctor."

"Thank you, Rance. And congratulations on your promotion, again."

"Thank you, again, Doctor."

Dr. Watson continued walking up the street and Rance walked around the corner.

Rance was able to find a hansom on the busier thoroughfare and immediately hailed one.

He told the cabby to take him to Scotland Yard and within half an hour Rance was on the steps of the new police headquarters.

Inside, the main access was as busy as it was on any other day. People waited to file reports or speak with a supervisor. Some were there to check the progress of cases already filed. Some were there to check on family or friends who were in custody. Rance enjoyed the out of doors work of being a policeman. Walking his beat. Meeting the residents in his patrol area. Knowing who belongs in the neighborhood and who is a stranger. Being cooped up in an office or worse, working the front desk, was not for him. He also enjoyed the responsibility of supervising the half dozen men under him in his patrol area. Still, it was sort of impressive visiting the new building; the paint still appeared fresh, the floors and staircases still shone as though they had been recently varnished.

Rance made his way to the upper floors where the inspectors had their offices.

Rance knew his way around the new building, probably better than any other sergeant. During his off-duty time he was constantly requesting case files to look over; especially those that weren't closed on the off chance he might find something overlooked by the original investigators. He wanted to see how the detectives handled certain cases. What they looked for or found when they searched for clues and evidence. He had studied all of the cases involving Sherlock Holmes, so he'd become familiar with some of the inspectors who most often worked with him. Lestrade was at the top of the list, but Gregson was a close second. Rance had looked hopefully at an opportunity of working with Lestrade on the Fairchild matter. Perhaps once Rance found him, they could share a carriage back to the Fairchild house and discuss the case.

Rance found the door to Lestrade's office and knocked loudly as a policeman would; a habit once developed which was almost impossible to break.

There was no answer.

Rance knocked again.

This time, Inspector Gregson came out of the office next to Lestrade's.

"Can I help you, sergeant?" Gregson asked.

"I was looking for Inspector Lestrade," Rance answered.

"He's out," Gregson explained. "Something to do with a break-in at a house in Kensington."

"I am aware, sir. I just came from there. Inspector Lestrade's not yet arrived."

"That's odd," Gregson said. "I'd say he left here some thirty or so minutes ago. We spoke briefly here in the hallway."

"This whole case is odd, sir," Rance said. "Been so from the beginning. What do you suppose has happened to Inspector Lestrade to delay him such?"

"Let's find out," Gregson said and retrieved his hat and coat from the hooks on the inside of his office then returned to Rance in the hallway.

"What are we going to do?" Rance asked.

In response, Gregson grabbed the doorknob to Lestrade's office and twisted. It opened right away.

"Lestrade?" Gregson called into the dark room.

There was no answer only the typical untidiness that was Lestrade's office.

"Well, for certain he's not in here," Gregson said. "Had to make sure."

"Good idea."

"Let's go downstairs and check at the front desk to see if the desk sergeant saw him leave," Gregson said and walked toward the stairs followed closely by Rance.

* * *

"Yes, sir," the desk sergeant responded to Inspector Gregson's inquiry. "Ordered his trap then watched him walk out about half hour or so ago. Right after I sent his telegram."

"Telegram?" Gregson asked. "Who'd he send a telegram to?"

The desk sergeant looked through a notebook on his desk until he came to the passage he needed.

"A Doctor J. Watson, sir," the sergeant affirmed. "Message was for the doctor to meet him at the Fairchild residence regarding strange circumstances."

Gregson processed this for a moment.

"Thank you, sergeant," Gregson said and stepped away from the sergeant's desk to allow him to return to his duties.

"Well, we know he left the building," Rance said. "Where to next?"

"Next will be to visit the carriage pool and find out who was assigned to transport the Inspector."

The two officers made their way out of the building and around a corner to where a stable was kept to house the police horses and carriages used by the detective squad.

"I think it was young Willie had been assigned to Mr. Lestrade today, sir," Reggie Hamm, the groomsman for the stables said after he was questioned by Gregson. Hamm was a tough man to work for. He ran his stables like an Army barracks. He was a short man but extraordinarily muscular and he had a weathered face that gave the appearance of both wisdom and age neither of which could actually be attributed to him. He enjoyed the company of horses over that of humans and he made no bones about it when it came to the drivers under his supervision. The horses under his charge were the best maintained in all of London. A fact Hamm was exceedingly proud of and a statement he was famous for making.

"Where is he now, Hamm?" Gregson asked.

"Should still be with the inspector, is my guess."

"The Inspector never arrived at his destination," Gregson stated.

"What?" the groomsman asked surprised. "Young Willie is one of the best horsemen we got here, sir. He don't lollygag or fool around none. He knows I don't put up with any of that guff. If'n he was told to transport Inspector Lestrade, then transport him he did. Here I'll shows ya. His carriage is missing."

Hamm took Rance and Gregson around to the back of the stables where the police carriages were stored for ready use.

"This is where young Willie keeps his carriage," Hamm said, "and it ain't here, so he must be with it."

At that moment a groaning noise came from a police carriage next to the vacant spot where young Willie's was normally kept.

"What was that?" Rance asked.

"Sounds like someone's hurt," Gregson said.

"Came from this carriage here," Hamm said and opened the door to the four-wheeler. Inside was a young lad of no more than twenty who was lying on his back on the rear seat and holding a hand to his head. He appeared to be nothing more than a wisp of a boy, maybe eight and a half stone soaking wet.

"It's young Willie," Hamm said.

"And not with his carriage," Gregson said with no attempt to cover the sarcasm. "Here. Move aside."

The groomsman stepped out of Gregson's path and Gregson moved toward the injured young man.

"Here, lad," Gregson said assisting the young man to a sitting position in the carriage. "What's happened to you?"

"I was coshed on the head," young Willie said holding a hand to the back of his skull. "I'da just finished hitching the horse to the carriage when I was struck. Didn't see no one. Hit me from behind, he did. Lousy blighter. Never even got a chance for a fair fight."

"Did he say anything to you?" Gregson asked.

"Nothing. Just hit me and dragged me into the carriage, just as I was...here now. Where's me growler? This'n ain't mine. Mine was right there."

Young Willie stood up but his legs wobbled and Gregson and Rance each grabbed an arm to assist him out of the carriage he was sitting in. He appeared to be quickly regaining his senses.

"My carriage was right here. It's gone now," Young Willie stated. "Blighter musta stole it."

"Who would be stupid enough to steal a police carriage?"

Hamm asked. "We got 'em all marked."

"What about Inspector Lestrade?" Gregson asked Young Willie ignoring the groomsman's comment.

"Never got to him," Willie said. "I was supposed to pick him up out front."

"He wasn't with you when you were struck?" Gregson asked a bit surprised.

"Naw," Willie said a little disgruntled. "Inspectors never come back here. We gotta drive round to get 'em. You should know that. I given you plenty of rides, I have, and never once did you walk back here with me."

Gregson was somewhat shocked by this veiled accusation. Inspectors did have a certain amount of indignation toward the lower ranks at times. However, until this incident, it had never occurred to him he appeared condescending to other members of the force.

"Maybe if'n Inspector Lestrade HAD been with me, I wouldn't have gotten this bump on me noggin and even if'n I had, the blighter would certainly be wearin' a pair of darbies right now, and my horse and carriage would still be here."

Young Willie was very upset and he went on for a few minutes more letting Inspector Gregson and Sgt. Rance know his feelings over being battered by an unknown assailant literally within feet of the greatest police force on the planet.

"We'll get you looked at by a doctor," Gregson said when Young Willie finished his rant. "Take this young man inside to my office and call for a doctor, will you Rance?"

"Yes, sir, but..." Rance said.

"But what, Sergeant?" Gregson asked.

"What about the call? The Fairchilds are still expecting

an inspector, Inspector."

"I suppose that duty will have to fall to me," Gregson said. "In the meantime, put out the word to all officers that a carriage and Inspector Lestrade have gone missing, and it looks like it may be the abduction of a police officer. I want descriptions of the carriage and of the Inspector given to every man on a beat. Can you handle that?"

"If I can't, I'll get a couple of the boys to help me, sir."

"Good man," Gregson said, and Rance walked off with his arm supporting Young Willie and guiding him back to the main building.

"Now," Gregson said to the groomsman, "I'll need another carriage and a horse for the trip to the Fairchilds' residence."

"Right you are, sir," Hamm said, then hesitated a moment. "Go back round the front, sir. I'll meet you there myself. If I don't show, or if someone arrives in my stead, you take him into custody in case whoever did that to poor Willie and absconded with Inspector Lestrade is intent on doing it again."

"Will do," Gregson said and made his way back through the stables and the building until he stood on the front steps of New Scotland Yard. It was about ten minutes later that Hamm arrived with the carriage and they were off in a shot to the Fairchilds' home in Kensington.

Chapter Five

"Disappeared?" Evert said once the slight shock of Gregson's news had worn off. "What do you mean? How could that happen?"

"We're not sure yet," Gregson explained, "but it's an odd thing. He was summoned here, we know. He sent a telegram to Dr. Watson to meet him here. He went for his carriage and his driver. Then, while waiting, the driver was clubbed over the head, the horses and carriage stolen, and Lestrade is now gone."

"Sounds more like a kidnapping," Watson said with actual concern in his voice. "This is terrible."

"I don't see the reason for his kidnapping," Gregson said. "That makes no sense to me at all."

"How so?" Watson asked.

"The Yard will never pay a ransom," Gregson explained. "Not for any inspector. Not for any sergeant. Not for any constable. We'd have officers being snatched hither and yon for money."

"Maybe it was something he was working on?" Evert said. "A special case."

"Plenty of those on Lestrade's desk," Gregson said. "Mine too, for that matter. And Jones. And Hopkins." **(6)**

"What are we going to do now?" Evert asked.

"Well, for now," Gregson said. "You're going to stand a post here in front of the Fairchilds' home. I'll get another constable to stand opposite at the back. I will want you men on regular patrol. Every thirty minutes you trade sides. Understand?"

"Yes, sir," Evert said. "Fresh eyes. Change of scenery so

we don't become complacent."

"Right," Gregson said with a smile. "You're sharp, Evert."

"Thank you, sir," Evert said and stood a little taller.

"That young girl would do worse not to involve herself with you."

"And what about me?" Watson asked.

"You, Doctor?" Gregson asked.

"Yes. I have no idea why I was even summoned here."

"That is strange," Gregson said. "Have you been in contact with Lestrade...I mean aside from your...recent loss."

"Yes, Inspector," Watson said the memory of Mary flooding back and displaying prominently upon his face.

"I'm sorry, Doctor Watson," Gregson said noticing the change to Watson's expression. "I didn't mean to..."

"Don't trouble yourself," Watson said but was clearly showing he was having some emotional difficulty.

"You're a friend of the Yard," Gregson said. "I'm sure Inspector Lestrade wanted to keep you included in some matters. For all the times you assisted us in the past."

"That really wasn't me," Watson offered regaining most of his composure.

"You were more of a help in those matters than you know, Doctor," Gregson said. "Your friend could be very condescending, and you seemed to buffer that between him and the Yard."

Watson nodded slightly.

"I invited Inspector Lestrade to dinner last night," Watson said. "To celebrate his success on a recent case."

"The frozen door?" Gregson asked.

"Yes," Watson answered. "That exact one."

"A remarkable bit of detective work, that," Gregson praised.

"That's precisely what I thought."

"Well, perhaps he was hoping to get another dinner," Gregson said with a smile.

Watson weakly returned the smile, but definitely saw the humor in the comment.

"Why don't you come with me," Gregson offered stepping to the carriage where Hamm patiently waited in the box.

"Are you sure?" Watson asked. "I'm not sure how much help I can be."

"Well, we'll see when we see," Gregson said and opened the door to the four-wheeler.

Watson entered the carriage and Gregson climbed in behind him.

"I'll get you another constable in a few," Gregson said through the window of the carriage to Evert who stood in front of the Fairchild house.

"Thank you, sir," Evert said. "I'll brief him as soon as he gets here."

"All right, then," Gregson said. "Hamm, take us back to the Yard."

Without a word, Hamm whipped up the horse and they all clattered down the street and around the corner.

Just around the corner, they came across another London Bobby, and Hamm pulled the carriage to the curb at Gregson's instruction.

"Here, Constable," Gregson said summoning the police officer.

"How can I help you, sir," the constable said then recognized the Inspector. "Oh, Inspector Gregson, I was sent to get you, sir."

"Me? What for?"

"They found the missing growler what was to transport Inspector Lestrade."

"What? Where?"

The constable gave the Inspector the address and he marked it down in his ever-present notebook.

"No sign of Inspector Lestrade, I gather?" Gregson asked.

"No, sir. Sorry, sir. But we're out searching. Ain't gonna rest til we finds him."

"I know that's how you feel, but I have another assignment for you for the next few hours, at least."

"I don't know, sir," the constable objected. "All the boys is out searching. Better to keep up looking for one of our own."

"Under normal circumstances, I'd agree," Gregson said. "However, this may actually be linked to the Inspector's disappearance."

Gregson told the young officer to meet with Evert at the Fairchild home to stand watch. The constable was visually disappointed in his new duties, but agreed to follow the order.

"Evert will brief you on the details and how to manage the surveillance," Gregson explained.

"All right, sir," the Constable said. "You'll send word once the Inspector is found, won't you?"

"Immediately, Constable," Gregson promised.

The constable walked away at a fast clip toward the Fairchild house. Gregson advised Hamm to proceed to the Yard.

"What do you think has happened to him?" Watson asked.

"I don't know," Gregson replied. "It has me worried."

"Why?"

"This kind of thing doesn't happen. We have a lot of crime in London; far too much in my opinion, but there is a respect for police officers. Kidnapping one? Well, Lestrade must be involved in something big."

"And he hasn't spoken to you about it?"

"No," Gregson said. "Not that I'm aware."

"What do you mean by that?" Watson asked.

"We discuss our cases quite often, so I'm aware of what he's working on, and he knows what I have on my plate. I can't recall him mentioning anything that would be so monumental as to warrant his abduction."

"What about revenge?" Watson asked.

"That's where I'm sort of leaning," Gregson said nodding in agreement. "I think I'll cable some of the prisons, Dartmoor, Reading and Newgate to start. See if any recent releases are men Lestrade was responsible for putting away."

"Good idea," Watson said. "What can I do?"

"I'm afraid, Doctor, I can't use your assistance in this matter."

"But back at the Fairchild's residence you said…"

"I know what I said," Gregson interrupted, "but that was for your benefit. I didn't want to embarrass you in front of Evert. It may be far too dangerous to involve an average civilian."

"You forget I was wounded in Her Majesty's service while in Maiwand and I spent a decade alongside Mr. Sherlock Holmes. I'm far from your average civilian."

"That all may be true, Doctor, but my superiors will never

see their way clear to allowing you to assist the Metropolitan Force. They weren't all that keen when Mr. Sherlock Holmes, himself, was involved. Politically, it made them look bad; inferior in a way."

"I promise not to make waves. I just wish to help."

Gregson looked sympathetically at Dr. Watson.

"I can't, Doctor," he said resignedly. "I'm sorry."

"We're at the Yard, Inspector," Hamm said from atop the four-wheeler as he pulled the carriage to the curb.

"Thank you, Hamm," Gregson said exiting the carriage. "Please take Doctor Watson to his home then come right back here, will you?"

"Yes, sir," Hamm said. "Where to Doctor?"

Watson gave Hamm his address in Kensington. It actually wasn't far from the Fairchilds' home and Hamm wondered why this route hadn't been followed first instead of traipsing all over London.

"Lestrade is my friend, too," Watson said before Gregson could enter the building. "I don't know how losing yet another person close to me will affect me."

"I understand, Doctor," Gregson said. "Honestly, I do. But think of this, if I let you assist and something were to happen to you, how am I supposed to live with that?"

Watson just stared at Gregson. He had no answer ready, but he wasn't about to let the matter drop.

"Go home, Doctor," Gregson said. "I'll send you frequent updates as they arrive."

Gregson turned and climbed the steps to the main entrance and disappeared into the practically new building.

"Shall we go, Doctor Watson?" Hamm asked.

"Yes, Hamm," Watson said dejected.

The carriage clattered away along the brick roadway. Watson took the telegram from his pocket and studied it. "Doctor. Need your assistance. Please meet me at the Fairchild residence. Lestrade," it read.

"Hamm," Watson said. "Take me to the Fairchild home. I want to ask a couple of questions before I go home."

"I don't know, Doctor," Hamm said. "I got my orders. I'm supposed to take you home."

"And you will, just as soon as I ask a few questions of the Fairchilds' cook. Then you can take me home."

"It sounds right out of the ordinary, Doctor. I don't think I shoulda be doing this."

"Fine. Take me home and I'll walk to the Fairchilds' residence. Either way, I won't be going into my house."

Hamm thought for a moment as the carriage clattered along the street. "I guess, it won't hurt none to take you to the Fairchilds'. This way I can keep an eye on you as well."

"Good thinking, Hamm," Watson said. "Gregson would be proud of your diligence."

Another twenty minutes or so passed and the carriage pulled to the curb at the Fairchilds' home. Dr. Watson exited the four-wheeler and encountered the young constable he'd met with Gregson the previous hour.

"Any word on Inspector Lestrade, sir?" the constable asked as Dr. Watson approached.

"Nothing, I'm afraid," Watson said and walked to the front door. "I'll just be a moment with the Fairchilds."

"All right, sir," the constable replied and went back to his post on the sidewalk.

Watson rang the bell and a long moment later it was opened by Lord Fairchild.

"Dr. Watson," Lord Fairchild said standing aside to allow Watson entry. "Have you come with some news?"

Watson entered the house and Lord Fairchild closed the door behind him.

"Not at the moment, Your Lordship," Watson said. "I was wondering if I could have a moment to speak with the young lady."

"I'm afraid not, Doctor," Lord Fairchild said. "We gave her that sleeping draft you provided, and she's been out for the better part of the last half hour."

"Hmm," Watson murmured. "She'll be down for the rest of the night, then. Well, allow me to give you my card. It has my address and hours on it. If she needs anything during the night, please don't hesitate to send for me."

Watson removed a business card from his vest pocket and presented it to Lord Fairchild.

"Thank you, Doctor," Lord Fairchild said taking the card. "I'll do that. It's very kind of you."

"You're quite welcome, sir," Watson said, then added, "How are the constables working out? Keeping things quiet?"

"They have been circling the house every fifteen minutes or so, but nothing has happened."

Watson nodded.

"Was there anything else, Doctor?" Lord Fairchild asked.

"No," Watson said. "I suppose not. Perhaps I'll have a word with Constable Evert before I take my leave."

"As you wish," Lord Fairchild said and opened the front door. "Good evening to you, Doctor."

"Good evening to you, Lord Fairchild, and the same to your lovely wife."

Watson exited the house and returned to the constable on the sidewalk.

"How long before you are relieved, Constable?" Watson asked.

"Any moment now, sir," the Constable answered then spied Evert rounding the corner. "Ah, here comes Evert now."

A moment later, Evert was standing in front of the Fairchild house.

"Anything to report, Simmons?" Evert asked the other constable.

"Nothing, Evert. You?"

"Nothing."

"I'll be off then," Simmons said and walked away in the direction Evert had come.

"We change positions often," Evert said to Dr. Watson. "Makes for less chance of boredom. Standing still can take a lot out of a person."

"I understand," Watson said.

"Have they found the Inspector?" Evert asked.

"No, they found the carriage, but there's been no sign of Inspector Lestrade," Watson said.

"Simmons told me about that, Doctor," Evert clarified. "I meant Inspector Gregson. Has he returned here with you?"

"No," Watson said. "It's just me. I wanted to stop in and see how Lydia was doing before I was escorted home."

"I see," Evert said. "And how is she?"

"Asleep, I've been told."

"That's good. She had a tremendous scare. It'll do her

good to sleep through the night."

"It will," Watson agreed.

"Anything I can do for you, Doctor?" Evert asked.

"I was just wondering why I had been called to this house by Inspector Lestrade," Watson said. "It really has me puzzled."

"You served in your capacity as a physician," Evert said. "That wasn't out of the ordinary."

"No," Watson said. "But how did Inspector Lestrade know I would be needed for that?"

"Begging your pardon, sir, but our inspectors are not as dim as the penny dreadfuls tend to portray them. If I were to go by the works of fiction, I'd swear the London Metropolitan Police couldn't find their own backsides with a lantern and a map."

"I've never made the London police look anything like that," Watson protested but not too forcefully. "Holmes had great respect for the officers of the law and he pointed out many of their strengths to me on the cases we shared with the police. Remember, he was a 'consulting' detective. They more often came to him for help. He didn't butt in on their work."

"Still, these fictional tellings go beyond respectfully describing our investigators," Evert said.

"You seem to know quite a bit about this so-called 'fiction,' Constable," Watson said with a wry smile. "Could it be you're a bit of an admirer of these tales?"

"You've got me there, Doctor," Evert said returning the smile. "I have to admit, I do enjoy a good yarn now and again. I like to imagine myself in the position of the detective and I try to see if I can solve the mystery before the fictional detective does."

"And how well do you do?"

"Not bad. More'n half I'd say."

"That's not bad at all," Watson congratulated Evert.

"Not in the league with your old friend, I'm afraid," Evert said a bit disheartened.

"No," Watson said. "But Holmes didn't start off as a great detective. He had to have made mistakes when he was first plying his trade. Can I assume you'd like to be an inspector someday?"

"It is my hope," Evert said. "But you also have to learn to play the game and I'm not much good at that."

"Play the game?" Watson asked confused.

"Politics," Evert explained a little disheartened. "Sometimes it's more of who you know than what you know. Still, I'd like to make a name for myself in some big case someday."

"Something like this Lestrade matter, maybe?"

"Exactly!" Evert said excited. "Can you imagine if I were able to find Inspector Lestrade? I'd be a hero and my profession would be set. Unfortunately, I am stuck with simple guard duty."

"Does anything come to your mind regarding the matter here at the Fairchild house?" Watson asked.

"Like what?"

"Evert, do you plan to use that object on your shoulders for more than a resting spot for your helmet?"

"Oh," Evert said. "I see your meaning. Have I thought about the intruder case while I was standing around out here?"

"Precisely," Watson said.

"I was thinking, why would someone break into a house for the sole purpose of frightening the cook?" Evert said.

"And have you come to any conclusions?"

"Not as of yet," Evert said dejectedly.

"Then you haven't thought hard enough," Watson admonished.

"That's not a fair thing to say, Doctor," Evert defended. "I've been giving this matter a whole lot of thought."

"Doctor," Hamm said from atop the four-wheeler. "We should be going."

"Give it some more thought," Watson said to Evert. "Then come see me after your shift ends."

Watson handed Evert another of his business cards. He then returned to the carriage and he and Hamm rattled down the street to the corner where they turned and disappeared from sight.

Evert looked at the card and was then interrupted by the approach of Constable Simmons for the post change.

"Anything?" Simmons asked.

"Nothing," Evert said. "You?"

"Nothing," Simmons replied. "What's that?"

"Dr. Watson's business card," Evert said.

"Dr. Watson? Like from those Sherlock Holmes stories?"

"The very man," Evert asserted.

Simmons was startled.

"That was THE Dr. Watson I was talking to?" Simmons asked.

"Exactly," Evert said. "Good fellow, he is."

"I wished I'da known. I woulda asked for an autograph for my missus."

Chapter Six

Dr. John H. Watson sat alone in his study. He tried reading a couple of articles from one of his many medical journals but could not concentrate enough to retain any of the information written on the pages. He'd placed the publication open across the arm of his easy chair and sat quietly listening to the silence broken only by the ticking of a clock on the fireplace mantel. His home was uncharacteristically quiet with Mary's absence. It was a heaviness on his heart. He was to a point where he almost hated to be at home. However, the London streets were not a better choice with the crime and the pollution. The yellow fogs could be as harmful as the influenza he'd battled against with so many of his other patients. It had been a hard winter and spring seemed to be taking its time in arriving.

Still, the good doctor knew he had to be home for the arrival of Constable Evert and any updates from Inspector Gregson. Watson saw a spark in the young constable, and he believed there could be great promise in the man as a police sergeant and even possibly an inspector if he truly applied himself and worked at increasing his knowledge base. He was also of the impression the constable was eager to make a name for himself and so would be willing to assist Watson in his investigations of Lestrade's disappearance.

The bell at Watson's front door rang, and Watson eased himself out of his chair making certain not to seem too eager to have company.

"Constable Evert," Watson said upon opening the door as if he were a bit surprised to see him. "Do come in."

Watson moved aside to allow the young police officer to

enter.

"I'm not bothering you, am I?" Evert asked stepping over the threshold and removing his police helmet.

"Not in the least," Watson replied with a smile, shutting the front door and directing Evert to the sitting room off the foyer. "Please have a seat."

The constable entered the sitting room and took a seat opposite the chair recently vacated by Dr. Watson.

"What made you choose that chair?" Watson asked.

"I'm sorry," Evert said rising from the chair. "I thought you were sitting there." He indicated the other chair.

"I was," Watson said. "Please sit down again. I was only wondering why you chose that chair to begin with. How did you know I was sitting in the other chair before you arrived?"

"From the magazine on the armrest," Evert said pointing at the medical journal. "I figured you'd been reading and got up when I arrived. I didn't want to take the chair you were already comfortable with. If I've somehow done something wrong, I apologize."

"Not at all," Watson said smiling. "It's good to see such intelligence in a young police officer. How long have you been with the force?"

"Not long," Evert answered. "Just a couple of months over two years."

Watson returned to his seat, and Evert sat back down in the one he'd originally chosen.

"I'm sorry," Watson said about to stand again. "Would you like a brandy or a whiskey?"

"I'll pass, Doctor," Evert said. "I'm afraid I can't stay long. I promised I'd put in a couple of extra hours off the books to assist with the search for Inspector Lestrade. Gotta have my wits about me."

"So there's been no news yet?" Watson asked relaxing into his chair.

"None," Evert said. "Oh, except they found the stolen carriage."

"I heard," Watson said. "Where was that?"

"Not far from your old stomping ground, actually," Evert explained. "Baker Street."

Watson covered his surprise with a slight cough.

"You all right, Doctor?" Evert asked.

"Yes, yes," Watson said. "Baker Street, you say? Close to 221B?"

"Actually, a street over. Not really ON Baker Street, but close enough that some of the boys mentioned how that was the area Sherlock Holmes used to live in."

"Have they searched the area?"

"Not as thoroughly as they'd like, but a good portion. So far, nothing. The thought is the carriage was dropped there to draw attention from where they're keeping the Inspector. The horse was probably taken to sell somewhere else. They thieves would find it difficult to sell a police carriage."

"Hmm," Watson murmured. "Strange they would pick that place of all of London, don't you think?"

"Maybe not," Evert said, thinking. "It could be a kind of calling card to the old days when Inspector Lestrade used to go to Mr. Holmes for assistance."

"Could be," Watson agreed.

"Could be it's just a coincidence, too."

"Anything new at the Fairchild house?" Watson asked.

"Nothing new there, either," Evert said. "Mighty strange that whole ordeal. I tried thinking on that the whole time I was standing my post and I can't imagine why that crime would have been committed. Not for the life of me."

"Are you sure of that?" Watson asked.

"Sure, I'm sure," Evert said. "I've been running Lydia's statements through my head all afternoon and evening. I can't figure out why someone would take the time to break into a house and threaten an innocent girl and make her fear for her life, but not steal anything or force himself on her."

"So you don't see any result in that act?" Watson asked.

"What do you mean?" Evert asked.

"After Lydia was terrified, what happened?"

"Nothing happened," Evert said puzzled. "Lydia stood still in the kitchen until Lady Fairchild arrived home with the baby. There was no theft, no damage, no attempt on Lady Fairchild or her baby or Lydia while the house was empty. Nothing."

"Something happened," Watson said attempting to guide the young officer along his path of thinking. "What was it?"

Evert thought for a while, then shook his head.

"Aside from the police being summoned, if something happened," he said, "I have no idea what it was. If you can enlighten me, please do."

"You almost had it," Watson said. "Inspector Lestrade was called to the scene."

Light began to dawn behind Constable Evert's eyes.

"You mean the whole incident at the Fairchild home was a set-up to get an inspector called to the scene and then to kidnap him?"

"I do," Watson said. "There seems to be no other explanation that would fit the facts we have so far, but it seems to me the abduction of a police inspector was the result of the intrusion. The criminals may have gotten away with something, after all, but not something from the Fairchild house. Something on its way TO the Fairchild house: the Inspector."

"That's amazing," Evert said, and Watson took a little pride in hearing it as he'd uttered it so many times upon hearing the reasoning of his illustrious friend. "It sounds exactly like something Sherlock Holmes would have come up with."

"Yes," Watson said, then added, "but I'm afraid he would have probably come to that realization within seconds of hearing about Lestrade's disappearance. He would have known right away the break-in at the Fairchild house was nothing more than a bizarre ruse to get an inspector assigned to the incident."

"You don't give yourself enough credit, Doctor," Evert said. "This is information the Yard should have. Would you mind if I delivered it for you?"

"Not at all," Watson said. "I'm happy to help."

Evert stood from his seat.

"Then I'll be on my way."

Watson stood as well.

"Thank you for stopping by, young man," Watson said. "Make certain Gregson and the other investigators keep aware of their surroundings. We can't know yet if Lestrade was the specific target or if this was a random abduction of any inspector."

"Perhaps there'll be more information at the station," Evert said making his way to the front door. "If there is, I'll send word back. If you don't hear from me, it's because nothing else has been learned."

"Thank you, Constable," Watson said following the young officer to his front door.

Watson opened his front door and allowed Constable Evert to exit.

"Good night, Doctor," Evert said replacing his helmet upon his head then made his way down the street at a quick pace.

Watson closed and locked his front door then walked back to his easy chair and resumed his seat.

It was only a moment before the silence of the house enveloped him once again and a strong feeling of melancholy washed over him.

"I'll wait a half hour," Watson told himself aloud. "Then I'll try for some sleep."

And Dr. Watson waited.

But no word came.

Chapter Seven

The next morning dawned with bright sunshine and a slightly higher temperature that promised warmer days in the near future.

Watson awoke in the easy chair he'd been sitting in with a slightly sore neck and a tightness in his lower back. He'd fallen asleep waiting for word from Constable Evert or Inspector Gregson, but obviously nothing had been forthcoming.

Slowly and achingly he rose from the easy chair and wondered silently why it was called an "easy" chair when he felt so uncomfortable from having spent the night in it. He made his way to his dressing room where he could get a change of collar and freshen up a bit. He had two appointments with new patients scheduled for late morning, and it wouldn't be a good impression for their new doctor to appear as if he'd lain out in the gutter most of the night.

Once refreshed, Dr. Watson prepared for his work day.

By early afternoon his medical duties were finished, and Watson felt some fresh air was in order. Actually he thought a nap was better suited due to his sleeping arrangements from the night before, but lying in bed without Mary was a difficult task unless he was physically exhausted.

Watson was far from physically exhausted. His emotions were more tired than his muscles.

He hailed a hansom and had the driver take him to the Baker Street Underground Station.

"Wouldn't ye rather I just took ye to the Kensington Station, guv'nor?" the cabby asked. "Ye could take the tube to Baker Street that way."

"I could," Watson said, "but I fancy a bit of fresh air. I don't mind the extra fee. And please, there's no rush."

"Right ye are, guv'nor," the cabby said, "If'n riding behind a horse is yer idea of fresh air."

The cabby whipped up the horse and they were on their leisurely way.

A short trip later from Kensington along Brompton Road near Buckingham Palace up to Marylebone and over to Baker Street, Watson was standing outside the Baker Street station fondly recalling the many times he and his famous friend used the station to travel to one part of London or another. They just as often used cabs, if not more so, simply because of their readiness.

Watson paid his driver who pocketed the fee and the healthy tip Watson provided, then stood by hoping for another fare from the departing passengers from the Underground. The cabby watched and shook his head in confusion as Watson slowly walked his way along Upper Baker Street; away from the underground station. "Why take a cab only to continue walking?" he wondered. "Lotta strange blokes in a city of almost 4 million people."

Watson walked casually up Baker Street until he came to his old lodgings at 221B. He stood on the pavement in front of the boarding house and gazed up at the first floor window where for years he'd shared rooms with his friend, Sherlock Holmes.

"They've set fire to our old rooms," Holmes had told Watson when he'd come to him at his home almost three years earlier. (7) Moriarty and his gang were hot on Holmes's trail, and he knew he had to get out of London – England actually. Inspector Lestrade and his team of police officers were clearing the streets of Professor Moriarty's gang of criminals. They had set fire to his Baker Street rooms in an attempt to destroy evidence Holmes had gathered against the gang. Unfortunately, for them, Holmes had already provided that evidence to Lestrade and the rest of Scotland Yard.

However, looking at 221B now, there didn't seem to be any damage at all. Whatever repairs had been made completely hid the fact that a fire had ever occurred there, at least so it appeared from the outside of the building. Perhaps the fire had been contained only to the interior of the structure? Watson thought.

The door to 221B suddenly opened and his former long-suffering landlady, Mrs. Hudson, emerged carrying some empty shopping bags. Watson stared at her while she turned to lock her front door and his heart filled with joy at seeing her again. She hadn't aged a bit from the last time they'd seen each other three years earlier. She was short but stout; a solidly built woman who had seen much in her life but wasn't the kind of person to share it. Her gray hair was thick and full and styled in the fashion of the day. Some wrinkles book-ended the blue eyes behind her glasses, but were a sign of having done much smiling and the lack of such wrinkles on her smooth forehead indicated she'd done considerably less worrying. There was no way to guess her age. She would never reveal it, and her quiet wisdom allowed for the assumption she was older than she appeared.

"Good afternoon, Mrs. Hudson," Dr. Watson said with a grin. "Out for a bit of shopping?"

Mrs. Hudson started at the call from the man in the street but when she moved her spectacles from where they rested on her head to their most convenient position, she immediately recognized the man who had spoken to her.

"Dr. Watson! Saints be praised!" she said smiling broadly, her Scottish accent becoming more pronounced with her exuberance over seeing her old tenant. "You are a sight for sore eyes, you are."

Mrs. Hudson shoved her shopping bags into the pocket of her coat and walked down the steps to throw her arms around her former tenant.

She embraced Dr. Watson in a tight hug, squeezing him without mercy.

"Mrs. Hudson," Watson gasped. "You're strangling me."

"Oh, dear," she said releasing Watson from her embrace. "Oh, I'm so sorry."

"No apology needed, Mrs. Hudson," Watson said. "I'm just as pleased to see you again."

"Won't you come in, Doctor?" she asked taking a couple of steps back to her front door. "I could put a kettle on."

"I don't want to impose, dear lady. I was just passing by. Besides you're obviously out to do your day's shopping. You must have the new tenants to tend to."

"New tenants?" Mrs. Hudson asked confused. "I've no new tenants, Doctor. No one since Mr. Holmes."

Watson looked puzzled at Mrs. Hudson.

"You know," he said returning the smile to his face. "I think I will come in for a few minutes if you truly don't mind."

"Nothing would please me more, Doctor," Mrs. Hudson said and returned to her front door where she quickly unlocked it and bade Watson to enter.

Inside, Watson spotted the seventeen steps that led to the first floor flat where he and Holmes had shared rooms and the beginnings of many adventures. **(8)** He recalled Holmes's chastisement for his not knowing the number of steps when he was trying to educate him on the use of observation. Watson had always believed that Holmes could just as easily have counted these steps a few moments before he posed the question about their number as he could have already known their number from having traversed them so often in the past.

Mrs. Hudson took the Doctor's hat and walking stick and placed them on the settee in the foyer. She hung her coat on the coat tree next to the door.

"Have a seat in the parlor, Doctor," Mrs. Hudson said pointing to the room next to the foyer. "I'll be but a moment to get the kettle going. Earl Grey all right with you, sir?"

"Earl Grey is just fine," Watson said. "And some of your biscuits and jam, if you have any?"

Mrs. Hudson smiled and dashed off toward her kitchen.

Watson looked around the parlor and even from the inside he couldn't see where there had been any damage from a fire or water damage from the fire brigade. The house looked exactly as it had three years previously when he'd last been with Sherlock Holmes. Perhaps the damage was in the rear of the house.

It was a conundrum, certainly.

Watson had resigned himself to walking up the seventeen steps when Mrs. Hudson returned.

"Fancy a look at your old rooms, do you?" she asked on seeing Watson staring up the staircase.

"I do, Mrs. Hudson," Watson said a little melancholy. "But I'm afraid it might bring back too many memories, and I've found those to be most disheartening at this time."

"Why is that?" she asked.

"You haven't heard of my wife's passing?" Watson asked.

Mrs. Hudson's face fell and her pallor whitened.

"I'm so sorry, Doctor," she said taking his hands in hers. "I never would have mentioned such a thing if I'd known. I am so sorry for your loss. How long ago?"'

"A little over a week," Watson said feeling the emotion creeping into his voice.

"Oh, Doctor," she said as tears filled her eyes. "I wish I could tell you you'll get over it, but the truth is I miss Mr. Hudson every day. The sorrow seems to fade and then there comes a day now and again when the sadness is just immeasurable."

Watson allowed his shoulders to fall while his hands gripped Mrs. Hudson's.

"But," she continued. "When I recall his memory nowadays it is mostly always with gladness. He put me up in this building by making investments that paid off greatly. I have two others. Did you know that?"

"Two other boarding houses?" Watson asked slightly surprised.

"Yes," Mrs. Hudson answered proudly. "One is run by my friend, Mrs. Turner. You remember her?" **(9)**

"From when Holmes and I first moved in."

"That's her. She manages the house on Marlene Road near the university. **(10)** I have another property out in Sussex."

"I never knew you were so wealthy," Watson said with a grin.

"Not wealthy, Doctor," she said with a bit of apprehension. "But comfortable. Thanks to my dear husband who long before his death took the care to invest for our golden years and not realizing he was providing for me prior to his untimely death."

Mrs. Hudson gazed up the stairs to the rooms rented by Sherlock Holmes so many years ago but she was obviously seeing a time when she was quite younger and her husband was at her side.

"Would you like to see the old rooms?" she asked after a moment's quiet reflection. "They've been kept just as they were when you and Mr. Holmes lived here."

"But...why?" Watson asked.

"Why what?" Mrs. Hudson returned.

"Why have you kept the rooms the way they were?"

"Because Mr. Holmes asked me to," she said.

Watson was stunned.

Holmes had to know he might not return from his trip to Switzerland especially with Moriarty on his trail. **(11)** All along Holmes knew he had a target painted on him by Moriarty and the members of his gang. He was a marked man back then; more out of vengeance than survival. Moriarty's empire had been destroyed. Holmes had provided evidence to the police to smash the whole criminal operation to bits. Moriarty had to flee London in order to save his own skin, but his hatred for the great detective far outweighed his need to survive. He would do anything and everything to end Holmes's life and on the cliffs over the Backbencher Falls, Holmes and Moriarty grappled until they both fell to their deaths at the bottom.

So why would Holmes have made assurances to keep his rooms as they were?

"You know Sherlock Holmes is not coming back, don't you, Mrs. Hudson?" Watson asked wondering if his former landlady was holding on to a misguided belief her old tenant would one day return.

"I do," she said not without sadness or hesitation.

"Then why follow his wish? Why not rent out the rooms to some other tenant?"

"It wasn't Sherlock Holmes's wish, Doctor," Mrs. Hudson explained matter-of-factually. "It was his brother's."

"Mycroft Holmes?" Watson asked. **(12)**

"Yes," Mrs. Hudson said. "He's pays monthly to keep the rooms as they are. Oh, I do a bit of dusting and airing out now and again, but otherwise all of his files and books and detective equipment are all still up there in his old rooms."

Watson looked back up the staircase. His mind was reeling with questions and suddenly he really wanted to see those old rooms.

"What about the fire?" Watson asked.

"Fire?" Mrs. Hudson said confused.

"Yes," Watson explained. "Holmes told me there'd been a fire in our old rooms on the night he came to me to ask if I'd accompany him to Switzerland. He said the Moriarty gang had set his rooms ablaze in a final attempt to destroy evidence against their master."

"There has never been a fire at 221B, Doctor Watson," Mrs. Hudson asserted. "I can take you up to your old rooms and show you."

Mrs. Hudson began climbing the seventeen steps up to the first floor. Watson hesitated for a moment then followed his former landlady to the rooms he'd shared with his famous friend.

"A moment, please, Mrs. Hudson," Watson said just as the lady removed her keys from her apron to open the door.

"Are you all right, Doctor?" she asked.

"Yes," Watson said. "It's...well...it's just been so long since I was here. I just wanted a moment...to prepare myself."

Watson nodded his head a second later to indicate Mrs. Hudson should unlock the door to his old flat. She pushed the door open and stood aside so Watson could enter.

Watson hesitated.

From the hallway, the room appeared exactly the same as the day he'd left to live with Mary.

Watson crossed the threshold.

The rooms appeared undisturbed, just as Mrs. Hudson had claimed.

They were cleaner and tidier than they had been when he and Holmes had lived there, but that was no doubt due to the actions of the dear landlady.

Watson looked fondly on the sitting room. Each item his gaze fell upon sparked numerous memories.

The chemistry table with Bunsen lamps and test tubes, a microscope and dozens of chemicals, (some labeled, some not, a dangerous habit but Holmes always seemed to know which was which) remained near the windows. The astounding filing cabinets with their records of cases (those handled by Holmes and numerous others handled by police agencies and detectives from around the globe) filled the wall next to the entrance. Holmes's commonplace books that held an encyclopedic amount of every day information from train schedules to registered pawn shop proprietors to shipping schedules were arranged on a bookshelf along with Holmes's scrapbooks which contained biographies of notable individuals, heads of state, celebrities and criminals as well as unsolved or mysterious events from the many newspapers he scoured every day for information. His collection of pipes was present as was the Persian slipper where he kept his tobacco. The jackknife he used to hold his unanswered correspondence to the mantel over the fireplace remained transfixed but there was no longer any correspondence trapped beneath the knife blade.

The sitting room chairs where Holmes would interview clients or listen to the problems of police officers and where he and Watson would discuss the events of a case or simply enjoy each other's company in quiet solace were still arranged next to the fireplace. Many were the times Watson would enjoy a good sea yarn while Holmes read a technical journal or involved himself in a personal study of some interest only to himself and his work. And, of course, it was in these chairs he'd first heard the story of a young woman who'd received a strange and lustrous pearl every year upon the anniversary of her birth for six years. A young woman whose concern for her missing father and the sender of the strange pearls would lead to the apprehension of a criminal and his deadly and horrific companion and a treasure of immeasurable wealth...and a marriage for the ages. It was where Dr. John H. Watson first met Mary Morstan and learned the true meaning of "love." **(13)**

It was the Baker Street of old. There was absolutely no indication of any damage or even the slightest bit of tampering. There was no way a fire could have blazed in these rooms other than in the grate and from the looks of the remarkably clean fireplace, that was a rarity itself.

Everything was just as it had been upon Watson's leaving.

But why would Holmes have lied to him? He wondered.

"You see, Doctor?" Mrs. Hudson said gently. "No fire. No damage at all. Everything is just fine."

But Watson knew everything wasn't just fine.

Something was definitely wrong and somehow Mrs. Hudson's boarding house had something to do with everything that was currently going on. Watson just had to focus his mind and see through the confusion to the solution of the puzzle.

"You're right," Watson said finally and smiled at this former landlady. "I must have misunderstood Mr. Holmes when he told me what had happened to the flat. Or perhaps, after these last few years, I simply misremembered what he actually told me. We all age."

Mrs. Hudson placed a sympathetic hand on Watson's forearm.

"We do indeed, Doctor," she said returning the smile.

"Although none of us do it with the grace and beauty you do," Watson said and bowed slightly.

"Oh, Doctor," Mrs. Hudson said blushing and swatting Dr. Watson's arm lightly with the hand she'd just been holding it with.

"We can go back downstairs, now," Watson said.

Mrs. Hudson led the way out of the flat and back down the staircase.

Once again comfortably seated in Mrs. Hudson's sitting room, Dr. Watson helped himself to some of Mrs. Hudson's biscuits and jam.

"These are absolutely delicious, Mrs. Hudson," he said of her biscuits.

"Thank you, Doctor," she replied. "I'd always thought I could have fattened up Mr. Holmes just a bit, if only he'd eaten more of my cooking."

"You always provided us a very healthy fare," he said.

"And delicious. I'm sure Mr. Holmes would have been more receptive had he been aware of just how talented you are in the kitchen."

"You're just full of flattery today, aren't you?" she asked with a smile.

"Not just today," Watson said and smiled as well.

Mrs. Hudson refilled Watson's tea cup from her pot.

"Now," Watson said becoming more serious. "You mentioned that Mycroft Holmes took over the rental of the flat?"

"Yes, Doctor," Mrs. Hudson said. "Right after the papers reported the death of Mr. Holmes, I received a telegram from Mycroft Holmes stating the rooms were not to be touched unless he was present and that all financial needs would be met at the first of the month to maintain the rooms. I'm sure he didn't mean for me to include you in keeping people out of the old rooms seeing you were Mr. Holmes's best friend and all. So I don't think there'll be a problem with you having gone up there."

"No," Watson said. "I can't imagine Mycroft having trouble with my little visit."

"Anyway," Mrs. Hudson continued. "Right as rain, at the first of every month I would receive the rent money sent by special messenger from the Diogenes Club. Why there? I don't have a clue."

"Mycroft was one of the founding members of the club," Watson explained.

"Oh," Mrs. Hudson stated with understanding. "That makes sense then, doesn't it?"

Dr. Watson nodded.

"And I've kept the rooms tidy and as undisturbed as possible for almost three years now."

"Have you tried to contact Mycroft in regards to Mr. Holmes's belongings and files and other personal items?"

"No, Doctor. When I first heard of Mr. Holmes's death I expected either you or someone would be around to pack things up and cart them off. When I got the telegram, I assumed that would be Mycroft Holmes. When I got the check for the first month's rent by special courier, I expected someone along the lines of a special courier would be along sooner or later. Now, it's been three years, and I've seen no one. I never met Mycroft Holmes and this is your first visit since the tragedy. Although, I can't imagine that was an easy time for you. Still, it might have been nice to have someone stop by for a visit."

"I am very sorry, Mrs. Hudson," Watson said with genuine sympathy and regret. "It was never my intention to exclude you from my life. I have no excuse for my callousness. I apologize and I promise to visit you once a month at the very least."

Watson smiled weakly, but genuinely.

"It has been good to have this visit," Mrs. Hudson said with less melancholy. "I'd love to have more."

Watson reached out and patted her arm reassuringly.

"So, in the past three years, Mycroft never once came by to check on his...investment?" Watson continued.

"Never once," Mrs. Hudson said. "I was beginning to think he intended the rooms to remain a shrine to his poor brother, but a shrine with no visitors isn't much of a remembrance, is it?"

"No," Watson agreed. "It isn't."

"I suppose if enough people had heard the story of the building being burned down, there would be no reason for a shrine and so no visitors to attend it."

"I suppose so," Watson said, but a thought began to tickle the back of his mind. Had Holmes known he wouldn't be returning? Had he taken precautions to make sure 221B wouldn't be trampled by ghoulish fans seeking a souvenir of some sort? How could he have been that aware of the future?

"Another biscuit, Doctor?" Mrs. Hudson said offering the plate to Watson.

"Oh, no thank you, Mrs. Hudson. You have been too kind as it is. I'm afraid I must be off, but I promise another visit soon. If that's fine with you?"

"I will look forward to it," she said smiling broadly.

Mrs. Hudson rose from her chair and walked to the settee in the foyer where she retrieved the doctor's hat and stick. She presented them to him as he stood next to the staircase leading to his old rooms and gazing toward the flat.

"Thank you, Mrs. Hudson," Watson said taking the hat and stick from his former landlady. "I will be back to visit soon. I promise."

"I will look forward to it," she said smiling again. "I'll walk you out, Doctor. I still have my shopping to do."

Mrs. Hudson removed her coat from the hall tree and opened the front door. Watson exited the boarding house and Mrs. Hudson followed immediately.

"One more thing, Mrs. Hudson. If I may?"

"What is it, Doctor?"

I understand there was some commotion on the street yesterday. Something about an abandoned police carriage. Were you aware?"

Mrs. Hudson shook her head.

"I did notice a number of constables down the street when

I went to do my shopping, but I'm afraid I didn't pay attention to the matter," she said. "Nothing serious, I hope."

"Well, yes, actually," Watson said. "Inspector Lestrade has gone missing, and the carriage he was in was found abandoned on Baker Street. We're all a little worried about him."

"Oh dear," Mrs. Hudson said concerned. "What do you suppose has happened to him?"

"No one knows yet, but we're all looking into the matter. I'm assisting in a small way."

"It's too bad Mr. Holmes isn't around," she said with a fond smile. "This would be just the case that he would love."

"It would indeed," Dr. Watson said moving down to the sidewalk. "It was good to see you again, Mrs. Hudson."

"And you too, Doctor," she replied. "Give me some advance notice for your next visit, and I'll have a proper lunch for you."

"I'll do just that," Watson said.

"Good day to you, Doctor," Mrs. Hudson said and turned to walk down the street to the market.

"And to you too, Mrs. Hudson," Watson said and walked off in the opposite direction.

Upon reaching the corner, Dr. Watson was startled by a four-wheeler that had suddenly pulled to the curb beside him.

The carriage was a black one with no markings and with a matching all black horse. The driver was bundled against an almost non-existent cold and so his face was obscured by a long, black scarf. Everything about this vehicle was dark and menacing.

The curb side door was flung open and a deep and extremely insistent voice came from the near complete darkness within.

"Get in, Doctor Watson," it said.

Chapter Eight

Doctor Watson peered into the interior of the four-wheeler. As his eyes adjusted to the darkness within, he recognized the occupant immediately.

Mycroft Holmes, Sherlock Holmes's more intelligent brother, sat in the rear seat of the carriage. His immense size taking up nearly all of the seat available.

"You may not realize it, Doctor, but you're in danger. I said 'Get in'." Mycroft repeated making his words sound more like an order than a suggestion.

Watson entered the carriage and took a seat opposite the enormous form of Mycroft Holmes. The carriage immediately began moving even before Watson could shut the door.

Mycroft reached over, grabbed the carriage door and slammed it shut leaving the two men in darkness except for where the daylight trickled through the cracks around the doors which wasn't much of a help in seeing the interior. The carriage windows had been completely covered with thick black curtains.

"What do you mean, I'm 'in danger'?" Watson asked.

"This matter with Lestrade," Mycroft said. "You are to drop it immediately. It does not concern you."

"He is my friend."

"Then, if you truly care about him, you'll excuse yourself from the investigation."

"Easier said than done."

"Well, do it all the same, Doctor. These are deep waters you find yourself in."

"How can I be in danger?" Watson asked suspicion dawning on him. "I've done nothing but assist another police inspector and be present at the scene of a strange occurrence; not even a real crime actually."

"I believe you were informed by that 'other inspector' not to involve yourself in this matter. And yet now you find yourself in the vicinity of where the police carriage was located." Mycroft said with an authority that comes from knowing what others do not know.

"I...I was visiting Mrs. Hudson," Watson stammered losing some of his confidence in his side of the conversation.

"After three years?" Mycroft asked with growing sarcasm. "You haven't seen fit to see the woman since the Reichenbach affair, but you expect me to believe you suddenly had an urge to visit her today? Doctor, you are as transparent as a window."

"Have you been watching me?" Watson asked surprised.

"There has been occasional surveillance," Mycroft conceded. "Off and on."

"For how long?"

"A while."

"As far back as Reichenbach?"

"Perhaps."

"Fine," Watson said. "I'll tell you why I'm involving myself. When your brother died, it was a terrible blow to me as I am sure it was to you."

Mycroft nodded slightly.

"He was the best and wisest man I've ever known," Watson continued. "But when I returned to London, I had my wife, Mary, to help me through the grief. Now, Mary is gone, taken from me just as viciously as if she'd perished over the same damn falls as Holmes did. And I have...I have..."

Watson was suddenly seized by emotion.

"I am truly sorry for the passing of your lovely wife, Doctor," Mycroft said, his tone completely changed to one of sympathy.

"Thank you, sir," Watson said regaining control of his feelings. "As I was saying, I've lost the two people who were closest to me. I have no intention of sitting idle while another friend meets his demise, especially if there is anything I can do to prevent it."

"Honorable intentions. However, you don't know what you're involved in. My position with the government will not allow me to jeopardize the safety of one of Her Majesty's subjects. You can understand."

Watson was suddenly seized with anger.

Who was this man to demand he stand down? Who was he to throw him in among the rabble of regular citizens? He, Doctor John H. Watson, late of the Fifth Northumberland Fusiliers, wounded in the service of Her Majesty at the Battle of Maiwand? How dare he?

"You can let me out now," Watson replied with barely controlled ire.

"I don't mean to offend you, Doctor," Mycroft said patronizingly, "but you really are out of your depth."

"I SAID LET ME OUT NOW!" Watson thundered and reached for the door.

The driver, having heard the demand, halted the four-wheeler and Watson jumped from the carriage.

"You have been warned, Doctor," Mycroft said.

"I've no need of your warnings, Mr. Holmes," Watson said his fury overflowing. "You sit behind a desk. You make

97

decisions that could cost lives, but you take no risk yourself. There is nothing you can say to me, no order you can bark at me, that will dissuade me from helping a friend. Good day to you, sir."

Without waiting for a reply, Watson stormed blindly off along the sidewalk not knowing where he was or what direction he was walking. He simply wanted distance between himself and the arrogant, pompous Mycroft Holmes.

The four-wheeler sped off in the opposite direction.

It wasn't until he'd reached the corner that Dr. Watson realized where he was and recognized his own block and his home a few houses in the across the street and in the opposite direction he'd been walking.

Taking a deep breath to regain his composure, Watson then crossed the street and made his way into his home.

Following a glass of whiskey and a few silent moments in his chair, Watson began to calm his senses.

"Danger," he thought. "What kind of danger? From whom? Damn that arrogant ass."

* * *

"That didn't go well," Mycroft told his driver through the trap door in the roof of the carriage once they'd rounded the corner and were a significant distance from where Dr. Watson had departed the cab.

"Indeed, it did not," the driver agreed.

"I thought his military baring would have allowed for me to order his compliance."

"It is just that sort of baring that makes Dr. Watson the man he is; blade straight and all that."

"He is an honorable man," Mycroft agreed without doubt.

"I'll give him that."

"Not many better in this city," the driver said.

"You'll have to continue to keep an eye on him, you realize," Mycroft said.

"Already planning for it," the driver agreed.

"Take me back to the office in Pall Mall, then prepare your surveillance. Send me updates through the usual channels."

"Yes, sir," the driver said and whipped up the horse to quicken the pace.

The four-wheeler clattered along the London streets toward the offices of Mycroft Holmes.

* * *

It seemed an eternity before the anger Watson felt began to subside. Those Holmes boys, he thought. How they must have tasked their parents.

This thought brought a slight smile to Watson's face. Imagining Holmes and Mycroft as children. Mycroft undoubtedly tormented his younger brother for being intellectually inferior and Holmes must have made light of Mycroft's eating habits.

They had probably been the two smartest men in London. The problem was, both of them knew that and the arrogance was palpable when in their company.

There was a knock on Watson's front door.

"If this is Mycroft Holmes again with another demand..." Watson mumbled as he rose from his chair to answer the summons. Already feeling his anger returning.

Upon opening his front door, he discovered to his pleasure his visitor was Inspector Gregson.

"Inspector," Watson said his demeanor improving

instantly. "Have you good news?"

"I'm afraid, no," Gregson said. "But on the uptick we've heard nothing bad either."

"Please, come in," Watson said and stepped aside to grant his visitor entry.

"Thank you, Doctor," Gregson said removing his bowler as he crossed the threshold.

"I was just having a glass of whiskey," Watson said ushering Gregson into the sitting room. "Would you care to join me?"

"I am on duty, Doctor, but a wee nip would probably do me good. I know it's spring time, but as evenings approach, there is a bite to the air."

Watson poured a bit more than a drop into a glass and handed it to Gregson who took a seat in one of the two easy chairs.

"What brings you here?" Watson asked resuming his chair and his glass of whiskey.

"I had to get out of the office," Gregson explained attempting to relax. "The walls were closing in on me so to speak."

"How goes the search?"

"Nothing new, as I stated, but we have every available man scouring the streets. It's only a matter of time. No one can hide forever from Scotland Yard."

Gregson gave a weak smile which informed Watson of just how exhausted the inspector was. It appeared as if he hadn't yet slept or even changed his clothing.

"You don't have every available man scouring the streets," Watson said light-heartedly.

"I appreciate your offer, Doctor," Gregson replied. "But I can't see my way to involving you."

Watson shrugged.

"You don't think he's run off on his own, do you?" Watson asked a moment later.

"No. No one believes that," Gregson replied. "We're quite certain he isn't faking his own disappearance. However, we've received no demand for ransom and no other communication."

"Could he be undercover on some assignment?"

"Unless it was something he'd come across on his own, no." Gregson said. "All of our supervisors have been queried regarding Lestrade's most recent orders and none of them admit to anything that would require him to vanish or go incognito."

"But if it was something of an extremely delicate matter," Watson offered. "Might your supervisors intentionally keep the information secret?"

"I suppose that's possible," Gregson said and rubbed his stubbled chin. "I hadn't thought of that, Doctor. "That is a good point. What made you think of it?"

"Mycroft Holmes paid me a visit," Watson said.

"Sherlock Holmes's brother?" Gregson asked.

"The one and only," Watson said and proceeded to enlighten Inspector Gregson with a recounting of the conversation he'd had with Mycroft Holmes.

"Were you in the area of Baker Street to check on the located four-wheeler?" Gregson asked.

"I was," Watson replied. "However, I discovered something much more interesting, but I'm not sure it connects with Lestrade's disappearance."

"What was that?"

"Holmes had lied to me."

"Lied?" Gregson said surprised.

"Yes," Watson said. "For some reason he told me the Moriarty gang had set fire to his rooms in Baker Street. But Mrs. Hudson told me that never happened."

"Why would he tell you that?"

"I don't know," Watson said. "The only reason I can think of is he wanted me kept away from Baker Street for some reason."

"Well, that worked," Gregson said.

"It did indeed. I haven't been to Baker Street since Holmes's death."

"But why wouldn't he want you there?"

"Again, I don't know, but I think his brother is aware of far more than he's willing to admit."

Gregson pondered this for a moment.

"What would you say to a visit to the man?" Gregson asked.

"You want to interview Mycroft Holmes?" Watson asked stunned.

"I do," Gregson said. "If he's hiding something and it involves Lestrade, I think the Yard has a right to that information. Any idea where we'd find him at this time of day?"

"The Diogenes Club in Pall Mall," Watson said. "But what about keeping me out of the investigation?"

"I've never met Mycroft Holmes. It might do me well to have you there for introductions."

"I'll get my hat," Watson said rising.

"Then, let's be off," Gregson said and drained his dram of

whiskey then stood up from his chair.

Watson marched toward the coat rack near his front door and grabbed his hat from the top hook with one hand while opening the door with the other.

"I'll be a moment," Watson said opening the door for Inspector Gregson to exit through.

"Are you all right?" Gregson asked.

"Yes," Watson said. "I'll meet you outside."

Watson shut the door on the surprised Inspector who walked slowly to the waiting four-wheeler.

Inside, Watson unlocked his desk and removed his old service revolver and placed it in his jacket pocket.

Back outside, Watson hurried to the carriage where Gregson stood patiently waiting.

"Let's go," Watson said.

The two men climbed into the police issued four-wheeler standing at the curb and Watson was happy to see the driver was once again Hamm from the Yard.

"Hello, Mr. Hamm," Watson said with a smile.

"Good evening to you, Doctor," Hamm replied. "Happy to have you with us again."

"Take us to the Diogenes Club in Pall Mall, will you, Hamm?" Gregson said following Doctor Watson into the carriage.

"Right you are, sir," Hamm said then allowed his passengers to settle before leaving the curb on his way to Pall Mall.

Chapter Nine

"What are you planning to ask Mr. Holmes?" Watson queried once the four-wheeler had started its journey.

"I'm going to flat out ask if he has any information that might assist the Yard in locating Inspector Lestrade," Gregson said. "If he's aware of anything he has to tell me. We can't keep using the services of every employee of the Metropolitan Police Force in the search for one individual; even if that individual is a police inspector. All of our other duties have fallen by the wayside."

"What about going to the press?" Watson asked. "Holmes use to praise the press for being able to disperse information he wanted sent out especially if it could result in misleading a suspect." **(14)**

"Do you suspect Mycroft Holmes in Inspector Lestrade's disappearance?" Gregson asked.

"No. Never. But..." Watson trailed off.

"But what?" Gregson asked.

"He sure seemed like he knew something. Something he had no intention of informing me about. Something, in fact, he seemed worried I'd somehow figure out. Or something he worried might come to light in front of the public."

"He believes this could somehow put you in danger?"

"He says so, but I'm not worried about that."

"Why not?"

"What reason is there for me to worry?" Watson asked. "I have work and nothing else. If my life were taken from me, who would be saddened by that fact?"

"Dr. Watson," Gregson said his voice overflowing with

concern. "You can't think that way. It's the path to self-destruction."

"Don't you think I realize that?" Watson said calmly. "Not a day goes by where I don't think about my great loss. I realize these are suicidal thoughts. I fight them. Continually. To be honest, if it weren't for the assistance I'd been giving Inspector Lestrade prior to his disappearance, I'm not sure how my life would be. If there'd even be a life for me...I'm sorry. I'm rambling."

"Not at all," Gregson said. "You need to feel as if you're necessary. Correct?"

Watson nodded.

"We all have that necessity," Gregson said. "It's difficult for me to imagine a day when I might leave the employ of Scotland Yard, but I know I'll have to at some point. It'll be up to me what I want to do with all the free time I'll have then. I'll plan for something."

"What if it happened tomorrow?"

"Why would I leave the Yard tomorrow? I have a long time left to work."

"My point exactly," Watson said. "I believed Mary and I had a lifetime left ahead of us. I'd always believed Sherlock Holmes would be at 221B Baker Street. Now, both are gone. I have my practice, but nothing to fill my idle hours. And there are many, many of those."

"What about all the cases you and Mr. Holmes worked on?" Gregson asked. "Surely, you've haven't written all of them up."

"Lestrade made the same suggestion a few days ago," Watson said with a smile. "Obviously, there are at least two people out there who would be interested in reading more adventures of the world's first consulting detective. Maybe I should get to work on telling some more of the old cases."

"There you are, Doctor," Gregson said sounding a little relieved. "Now, let's have no more of this melancholy. Promise me, if you start thinking sour thoughts, you'll come find me."

"All right, Inspector," Watson agreed with a weak smile.

"All right, what?" Gregson asked.

"I'll come see you," Watson said.

"Promise?"

"I promise," Watson said and raised his right hand in oath.

"Good."

"Diogenes Club," Hamm called from the roof of the carriage as he pulled to the curb.

Watson and Gregson exited the four-wheeler and stepped onto the busy sidewalk. Londoners walked quickly back and forth in front of the building.

Watson and Gregson excused their way to the entrance to the strangest club in London; the Diogenes. It was a non-descriptive brick building. The few windows with views upon the street were shuttered save for one. There was a tiny plaque designating the edifice as "The Diogenes Club" and it was partially hidden by a bell pull next to a large black wooden door. It was almost as if the founders of the club didn't want any attention brought to their location.

Which would make sense since Sherlock Holmes had informed Watson that his brother started the club so the most unclubbable men of London would have a place to go. However, these men never spoke to each other. There was only silence in the Diogenes save for an area know as The Stranger's Room. It was the only room outside of the front desk area where anyone could speak. **(15)**

Ignoring the bell pull, Inspector Gregson, followed by Dr. Watson, walked inside and directly to the front desk which was stationed by a retired military man named Geoffries who sported a graying mustache and thick mutton chop side whiskers and was attired in what appeared to be a dress military uniform although no rank or insignia appeared anywhere upon it.

"May I assist you, gentlemen," Geoffries said obviously perturbed at having the front bell ignored by these two strangers and capable of maintaining an attitude that gave the impression he wanted to do anything else but assist.

"I'm Inspector Tobias Gregson of Scotland Yard," Gregson said and produced a police identification. "And this is Dr. John Watson. I'm here to ask Mr. Mycroft Holmes some questions, and Dr. Watson is an acquaintance of his."

"I see," Geoffries said transferring his piercing gaze from one man to the other. "A moment."

Geoffries jotted down a note and rang a small bell on the desk in front of him. Not even a moment later a young lad of about eight and dressed in a smaller but similar uniform appeared almost out of thin air and stood at attention before Geoffries.

Due to the near military aspect of the situation, Watson expected the boy to salute but no such action was taken.

"Take this to Mr. Holmes," Geoffries said and both Gregson and Watson spotted a flicker of fear cross the boy's face. "Wait for a response."

"Yes, s-sir," the boy stammered but very slightly and a moment later he was gone with a speed that was nearly supernatural.

"It will be but a moment longer gentlemen," Geoffries said. "Are you familiar with the rules of this club?"

"I am," Watson said.

"I've never been here," Gregson replied.

"We don't allow speaking," Geoffries said ignoring Watson's response. "If you somehow are allowed in and you speak anywhere outside of the Stranger's Room, you'll be escorted out of the building and there will be no further entrance."

"I'm a police inspector, not a member of the club," Gregson reiterated.

"It doesn't matter," Geoffries stated emphatically. "Once you leave this foyer, you are subject to the rules of the club; members or not. Do you understand?"

Gregson nodded and turned to look at Watson whereupon he rolled his eyes.

Watson suppressed a slight chuckle by covering it with a false cough.

Geoffries wasn't fooled.

The boy returned pale and with eyes wide with terror at having to meet with Mycroft Holmes. He handed Geoffries the note.

Geoffries took the note, nodded to the boy who then disappeared with great relief.

After glancing over the note, Geoffries said, "Mr. Holmes declines your request. He asks that both of you leave immediately and advises there are two police superintendents currently among the club membership and presently in attendance who will make certain you comply with his wishes."

Geoffries stared directly at Gregson upon finishing his

statement and only a head nod toward the club's entrance was added to the conversation.

Gregson stared a moment longer then turned and left followed quickly by Dr. Watson.

Once on the sidewalk in front of the Diogenes Club, Watson placed his hat back on his head and Gregson looked at the door that had just figuratively been slammed in their faces.

"That didn't help," Gregson said.

"Are you sure?" Watson asked.

"What do you mean?"

"Obviously we've stepped on some cat's tail," Watson said with a smile. "Why be so obstinate if there's nothing to see? Mycroft must know something."

"How do we find out what it is, then?"

"We take another avenue," Watson said but truly having no idea where to go.

"You mean checking into what Lestrade was working on?" Gregson suggested.

"As good a place to start as any," Watson agreed.

"Then I guess we're off to the Yard," Gregson said and climbed into the four-wheeler with Watson a moment behind him. However, just before he climbed into the carriage, Watson glanced up at the windows above the front entrance to the Diogenes Club and was certain he saw the curtain move slightly in the one that wasn't shuttered. Believing so, he tipped his hat and got into the carriage.

After the four-wheeler had moved away from the curb, Gregson asked Watson, "What was that about?"

"What was what about?" Watson asked.

"Tipping your hat?"

"Mycroft Holmes claimed the view from his office was a wonderful vantage point in which to observe all types of humankind. **(16)** I figured he was using that vantage point to watch us leave."

"And was he?"

"I believe so, I didn't actually see him, but I think I detected a slight movement of the curtain. This would be just like Mycroft to signal he was aware of us."

"Hamm!" Gregson called from the interior of the four-wheeler and a moment later the small trapdoor opened on the roof of the carriage and Hamm's face appeared.

"Yes, Inspector?" Hamm asked.

Maintaining a low speaking voice, Gregson said, "Keep a sharp eye, will you Hamm? We might be followed. If we are, I want to know about it, but don't try to shake him and don't give away that you know anyone's there."

"Will do, sir," Hamm said and shut the trap door and a moment later the carriage began to move.

"You think he'll put a tail on us?" Watson asked.

"If he's anything like his brother, I wouldn't put it past him," Gregson said. "Although, I have to admit, we're probably more in the dark than he is regarding the Lestrade matter."

"So it wouldn't do him any good to know what we know because we obviously know less that he does," Watson said.

"Confusing, but true," Gregson said.

The two men rode on in silence; each lost in his own thoughts.

111

Chapter Ten

The police carriage pulled to a stop at the main entrance of Scotland Yard, and Gregson and Watson alighted and stood together on the sidewalk.

"See anyone following us?" Gregson asked Hamm.

"No one, sir," Hamm replied uncertainly. "Though traffic was pretty heavy. I could've missed someone."

"All right," Gregson said.

"However, I'm fairly certain if someone was behind us, it wasn't for any great piece," Hamm said.

"Good man," Gregson said. "Keep the horse and carriage ready, will you Hamm? I might be in need again soon."

"Aye, sir," Hamm said and drove off to return the carriage to the lot behind the Yard.

"I thought we could go up to Lestrade's office and go through the cases he was handling," Gregson said as he escorted Watson into the building. "We can check through his files to see what he was most recently assigned to."

Watson followed the inspector deeper into the building and up the stairs to the offices of the police inspectors.

"I know you've been here a number of times since the new building opened, but better let me handle things in Lestrade's office," Gregson said. "It wouldn't do for someone to catch you going through police files even in my presence."

"Agreed," Watson replied.

The two men entered the cramped, dingy office assigned to Inspector Lestrade. The windows were still shuttered which added to the gloominess of the room. There was a small desk with a lamp upon it and two chairs; one behind the desk, presumably Lestrade's, and one in front of the desk. Of the two, only the one behind the desk appeared to offer any comfort.

"Did he like it dark in here?" Watson asked noticing the windows were shuttered.

"I'm not sure," Gregson said and walked over to the windows to open the shutters. "He might have. All Inspectors have their little habits. I occasionally like to remove my shoes while I'm sitting at my desk."

"I do the same thing while I'm writing," Watson said with an understanding smile. "If I have shoes on I always feel like I'm supposed to be going somewhere and if I'm barefoot...well...that's just comfortable."

"So, it wouldn't be out of the ordinary if Lestrade wanted it dark in here," Gregson said. "Perhaps seeing the out of doors was too much of a temptation for woolgathering. He may have closed his shutters to block out distractions."

"That's sound enough," Watson agreed. "What should we be looking for?"

Gregson was already searching over the top of Lestrade's desk, moving some papers and files but doing his best not to disturb anything that wasn't necessary to the search.

"I'm looking for his daily log," Gregson said. "It's possible he had it with him when he disappeared, but I doubt it. It might be here. That would make things infinitely easier when searching his hours prior to the last time he was seen. We're all supposed to keep one of those logs, but as far as I know, I'm the only one of the inspectors who does maintain one with any regularity. It helps me with organizing my cases and is useful when I'm testifying in court, but I can't seem to find Lestrade's here."

"You said he might have had it with him." Watson said. "You know, when he disappeared."

"Possible, but unlikely," Gregson answered. "Mostly we kept them here in the office and filled them out at the end of the day. At least that's how I do it. I transfer all of my notes from my personal notebook into a more coherent form in my log book. Maybe Lestrade maintained his in a different manner."

Watson began to examine the bookshelves in the tiny room. One wall held the shelves while the opposite displayed a line of filing cabinets.

"Is this it?" Watson said plucking a notebook from where it rested atop several dusty volumes on British Law. He handed it to Gregson.

The notebook had the London Constabulary crest on the cover and it was tied shut with a leather strap. It looked as though it had never been opened.

"Looks exactly like the one I keep my notes in," Gregson said taking it from Watson.

A look of stunned surprised crossed Gregson's face upon opening the notebook.

"It's blank," he said flipping backward and forward through the pages.

"How can that be?" Watson asked a little surprised. "Is it new? Perhaps he'd already filled his last one and was going to be starting on a new one?"

"I don't think so," Gregson said. "We were all issued the same type of notebook a little over three months ago. There's no way we've done enough to fill one of these and start a new one. I'm not even a third of the way through mine."

"Perhaps he never used his," Watson offered.

"It seems that way. We'll have to look elsewhere to find what he might have been working on."

"What did you find on his desk?" Watson asked.

"Some notes on the burglary case he cracked," Gregson said. "A couple of initial reports on suspicious persons. Nothing major. Nothing that mentions the Diogenes Club or Mycroft Holmes, if that's what you mean."

"Well, I didn't expect for there to be a large file labeled 'Dire Situation'," Watson said a little too sarcastically. "Sorry about that. I didn't mean..."

"It's all right," Gregson said reassuringly. "We're all a little on edge."

"Thank you."

The two men continued to search the tiny office but to no avail.

"Well, we've learned one thing," Gregson said when they'd finished searching.

"What's that?" Watson asked.

"Lestrade is a slob," Gregson answered.

Watson couldn't help but laugh.

"I'm sure he knows where everything is," Watson said. "Holmes was also a very untidy fellow, but he could locate the smallest piece of information from his stacks of files within seconds."

"If only we had a method to Lestrade's madness, then. None of his current cases would warrant his kidnapping," Gregson said. "Why would someone abduct a police inspector?"

"I've no idea," Watson said and sat down heavily in the lone chair in front of Lestrade's desk.

He'd been correct in his assessment of it.

It was not comfortable.

"Perhaps we're missing something," Gregson said.

"We have to be," Watson agreed and glanced around the room again. "But what?"

"I guess if we knew we wouldn't be missing it."

"Maybe we're in the wrong location."

"This is the only office he has," Gregson said.

"Where else do you work?" Watson asked.

"I sometimes work from home," Gregson responded as realization dawned on him. "That's got to be it. He must have been working on something sensitive; too sensitive to simply leave it lying around here at work."

"Did anyone search his house after his disappearance?" Watson asked.

"Yes, but we were looking for him, not any of his cases," Gregson said. "Once it was determined he wasn't at his home, his rooms were secured and the officers left."

Watson stood up from his chair.

"Shall we?" Gregson asked.

"We shall," Watson answered feeling good to be a part of some investigation again. Then it dawned on him that this inquiry could lead to more bad news; devastating news if the worst had happened to Lestrade, in fact, and some of the excitement left him.

"Meet me out front," Gregson said. "I'll summon Hamm and his four-wheeler."

Watson needed no further prodding. He was out the door and headed down the front stairs to the main entrance.

Chapter Eleven

"I'll wait right here for ye," Hamm said pulling up in front of Lestrade's residence.

"Thank you, Hamm," Gregson said climbing out of the four-wheeler followed immediately by Dr. Watson. "I don't know how long we'll be, so if you're hungry and want to get yourself a little something, please do so."

"Thank you, Inspector," Hamm said. "I think I'll do just that. Be back in about fifteen, then, sir."

Gregson nodded and Hamm took the four-wheeler from the curb and rounded a corner half a block away.

Gregson and Watson approached the front door. Gregson was about to knock when he noticed the door wasn't completely shut.

"What's this?" he asked looking at the slightly ajar front door. "The weather's still too cool to be leaving doors or windows open."

"Best knock anyway," Watson suggested.

Gregson rapped his fist on the front door and the door opened inward. Silence responded to his knock.

"I don't like this," he said.

Watson nodded in agreement.

"You'd better wait out here," Gregson told Watson. "Safer."

"For whom?" Watson asked.

Gregson smiled and nodded and the two men cautiously entered the boarding house.

"Hello?" Gregson called. "Police officers."

Watson smiled slightly at being included in the Gregson's

identification.

"Inspector Gregson of the Yard. Is anyone at home?"

There was no answer to either of the Inspector's calls.

"We seem to be alone," Gregson stated.

The two investigators slowly made their way into the house. In a sitting room off the entrance, they discovered a gray-haired elderly woman in a plain blue house dress lying on the floor.

She was unconscious. There was a bruise on her forehead slightly below the hairline, but she was covered by an afghan and her head was raised by a throw pillow tucked beneath it.

"That's Mrs. Lynch," Gregson claimed in a quiet voice. "She's Lestrade's landlady. Who would have done this to her?"

Watson knelt by her side and felt her delicate wrist for a pulse. He then placed two fingers against her throat and pulled his watch from his pocket and proceeded to count heartbeats.

"Her pulse is strong and her breathing is steady," he said in a hushed tone. "She's been out for a while for a bruise of this size to have formed."

"Can you do anything for her?" Gregson asked.

"She seems fine, but I'd better wait until she regains consciousness to make a more accurate diagnosis of her condition. Help me get her off the floor and onto the settee."

The two men lifted the elderly woman and placed her frail body on the settee where Watson once again covered her with the afghan and placed the pillow beneath her head.

"All right, then," Gregson said. "You stay with Mrs. Lynch and I'll go check the rest of the household."

Watson nodded in agreement.

Gregson left Watson in the sitting room alone with Mrs.

Lynch and made his way up to where Lestrade's rooms were located at the top of the stairs.

The stairs creaked as he slowly climbed them, instantly giving away his location, and he silently cursed the otherwise quiet of the house.

The door to Lestrade's rooms showed signs of having been forced. Gregson pushed on the door and a low squeak came from the hinges as it opened.

The room was dark. The drapes had been pulled shut except for a sliver where they nearly met in the middle of the main window and bright sunlight streamed through. It took a moment for Gregson's eyes to grow accustomed to the darkness and the contrasting but focused beam of sunlight, but in that moment he suddenly realized something.

He wasn't alone.

* * *

In the sitting room, Mrs. Lynch began to stir. She moaned deeply and lifted a hand to her head. She winced with pain when her hand touched the area with the bruise.

"Oh my," she said painfully, feeling the bump that was growing on her forehead.

"I'm Dr. Watson, Mrs. Lynch," Watson said from an overstuffed chair he'd drawn up next to her. "You've received a head injury. How are you feeling?"

"Dr. Watson?" she murmured. "How...?"

"I came here with a police officer," Watson explained.

"Mr. Lestrade?" she asked hopefully and tried to sit up. A severe wave of dizziness swept through her causing her to nearly pass out again.

"Please don't tax yourself, Mrs. Lynch," Watson said and

got the woman to lie back down on the settee. "It is Inspector Gregson I am accompanying. We're looking for Mr. Lestrade. Who did this to you, Mrs. Lynch?"

"I...I don't know," she stammered and an expression of confusion crossed her face. "I was making tea, when the bell rang. I've been so worried about Mr. Lestrade. It's not like him to stay out for so long, and the officers who came here looking for him two days ago said no one had seen him. I was hoping it was he who was at the door. He occasionally forgets his key."

Watson smiled at this.

"Who was at the door?" he asked.

"I don't know," she responded. "I answered it and that's the last thing I remember. Until I woke up here in the sitting room, that is. Ooh, my head. What happened to me?"

"It seems someone broke in and coshed you on the forehead, Mrs. Lynch," Watson explained. "Can you tell me how you feel otherwise? Are you experiencing pain anywhere else besides your head?"

"No, nothing," she answered. "I'm fine, I suppose. A little weary, some aches, nothing that doesn't already come with old age."

"Well, I'm sorry about your aches, but it's good there's nothing else," Watson said reassuringly. "Please try to rest. I'm sure Inspector Gregson will want to ask you some questions."

"OH MY!" Mrs. Lynch blurted out suddenly. "The kettle. I left it on the burner!"

"I'll take care of it, ma'am," Watson said and left her to go to the kitchen.

In the kitchen, the kettle sat on a cool burner on the stove. It was still full of water. Watson returned to the sitting room.

"No worries, Mrs. Lynch," Watson said. "The kettle is fine. The burners are all cool."

"But, I didn't take the kettle off the burner," Mrs. Lynch objected. "I'm surprised the whole house didn't burn down."

"Perhaps you did and you simply don't remember it," Watson offered.

Mrs. Lynch wrinkled her brow as she struggled to recall her most recent memories.

"No," she said. "I may be old, but my memory's as good as ever. I'm certain I didn't take the kettle off the burner. Someone else must have done it. Mr. Gregson, perhaps?"

"He never went into the kitchen," Watson said. "When we arrived, your front door was left ajar, so we entered. We actually found you lying on the floor with that afghan covering you and that pillow beneath your head. You don't recall anyone else assisting you?"

"No one, Doctor," she said. "I remember the bell ringing and then you. Nothing in between."

"That is odd," Watson said and began to ponder what had occurred in the last hour or so that would have resulted in Mrs. Lynch being administered to in such a fashion.

Mrs. Lynch looked questioningly at Dr. Watson.

"You're not..." Mrs. Lynch began.

"The Doctor Watson from the Sherlock Holmes stories," Watson finished with a slight smile.

"Yes," Mrs. Lynch said eagerly.

"One and the same, I'm afraid," Watson said.

"Oh, how thrilling," Mrs. Lynch said and some much needed color returned to her cheeks.

*   *   *

In Lestrade's rooms Gregson's eyes had grown accustomed to the dimness. The figure stood between the sunlight streaming through the thin gap between the drapes and Gregson near the door. There was no discernible description of the person in the room with Gregson as he was seen only in silhouette but the revolver in his right hand was easily illuminated by the sunlight almost as if the intruder intended for Gregson to see it clearly.

"I had nothing to do with the attack on the landlady," the shadowy intruder said matter-of-factually and in a gravelly whisper. "I had nothing to do with the disappearance of Inspector Lestrade for that matter."

"No one has accused you of anything," Gregson said allowing his police training to take over and sounding more calm than he actually felt. "In fact, other than threatening the life of a police officer with a firearm, I can't say you've done anything else wrong. Maybe a little trespassing, but both of those things can be excused if you're willing to talk with me. How about putting the gun down?"

"I'm not the culprit here," the silhouette stated. "I don't have time to sit and chat. I have work to do. Now, if you'll be so kind as to turn your back..."

"I won't do that," Gregson said. "I'll not give you the opportunity to shoot me in such a cowardly fashion."

"I have no intention of shooting you, Inspector. If I had, you'd be dead already and I'd be on my way with no one the wiser."

"Then why should I turn my back?"

"I must leave," the intruder said. "I don't want you seeing me."

123

"I can't let you leave the scene of a crime," Gregson said. "Not without answering a few questions. If you have nothing to hide, as you state, put down the gun and let's talk about this."

"I'm afraid that's out of the question," the shadowy figure stated. "You will turn your back or you will receive a bullet graze to the side of your left leg. It won't be fatal, but it will incapacitate you long enough for me to escape. How shall we proceed?"

The stranger adjusted the aim of the revolver toward Inspector Gregson's left thigh and steadied his grip.

Gregson realized this person was serious and slowly turned his back to him.

A moment later the drapes were flung aside and the window was raised.

"Good day, Inspector," the figure stated and a moment later was gone.

Gregson turned an instant after that but had to shield his eyes from the blinding sunlight. The delay allowed the stranger to disappear from immediate view. By the time Gregson was able to get to the window there was no sign of the intruder.

The street below was empty save for the police four-wheeler and Hamm sitting upon it and eating the contents of a newspaper cone of fish and chips. The ledge outside the window and the small yard in front of the building were all empty.

"HAMM!" Gregson called to his driver.

Hamm turned in his perch and looked in the direction of the house but it took him a moment to locate Inspector Gregson waving from the first floor window.

"Anyone pass you in the last few moments?" Gregson called.

"No one, sir!" Hamm called back.

Gregson disappeared back into the building.

* * *

Having heard the yelling from the sitting room, Dr. Watson got up from his chair next to Mrs. Lynch and walked over to the staircase.

As he was about to mount the stairs, Inspector Gregson appeared and ran down the steps two at a time. He raced past Watson to the front door and out into the open.

Gregson looked up and down the street, then back to the house.

"What happened, sir?" Hamm asked from his perch and glanced around himself.

"There was an intruder," Gregson walked over to Hamm at the curb and continued. "He held me at gunpoint then escaped through the window whence I called to you."

"I saw no one, Inspector," Hamm said. "I swear. If'n I had, I certainly would've brought attention to him."

"You're positive no one passed you?" Gregson asked.

"Yes, sir."

"Were you watching the house?"

"Well...no sir," Hamm said. "I didn't know I was supposed to be watching it, sir."

"So someone could have exited through the window without your notice then?"

"I suppose so."

"Or climbed to the roof of the house?"

"Yes."

"What's happened?" Watson asked as he joined Gregson and Hamm at the curb.

Inspector Gregson provided Watson with a brief account of the last few minutes and his encounter with the armed shadowy suspect in Lestrade's rooms.

"How terrifying," Watson said.

A shriek of terror came from the interior of the house.

Watson, Gregson and Hamm raced into the building and to the sitting room where Mrs. Lynch now sat upright on her settee pointing at her kitchen.

"A man!" she wailed. "He ran through here and into the kitchen. I heard the back door slam. He came from upstairs."

"Stay with Mrs. Lynch," Gregson ordered Hamm and dashed through the kitchen followed closely by Dr. Watson. They wrenched open the back door and raced into a much larger backyard than that of the front. No one was about.

A short picket fence separated the yard from an alley behind the house. The yard was empty and the alley was just as desolate. There was no one in the area.

"Again!" Gregson said and slapped his hand against his leg. "Damn!"

"Should we search for him?" Watson asked.

"Where would you suggest we begin?" Gregson said. "Perhaps we could look for the puff of smoke he disappeared into?"

"I'm only suggesting…" Watson said.

"I know, Doctor," Gregson interrupted much less sarcastically and patted Watson on the arm. "I'm sorry. This has been very frustrating, and I was foolish enough to fall for the intruder's deception. It's my fault."

"Don't blame yourself," Watson said. "If I'd stayed with Mrs. Lynch, I could have grabbed him."

"He had a gun," Gregson debated.

"As do I," Watson said patting the pocket of his jacket.

"I'd much rather have this not turn into something out of the American Wild West," Gregson said.

"But you said he pointed a gun at you," Watson countered. "Why point it if he wasn't planning to use it?"

"He was just using it to keep me at bay," Gregson said and quickly told Watson of how the intruder only made a threat to shoot him in the leg. "I don't believe I was actually in any danger."

"And you also don't believe he was responsible for striking Mrs. Lynch?"

"Nor that," Gregson said. "Based on how we discovered her, I think he rendered aid to Mrs. Lynch."

"Well, there's no doubt someone assisted her prior to our arrival," Watson agreed and told Gregson about the kettle being removed from the stove burner.

Gregson led the way back into the house.

In the sitting room, Hamm had already assisted Mrs. Lynch into a more comfortable position on the settee.

"Did you find him?" she asked Dr. Watson and Inspector Gregson upon their return.

"No, ma'am," Gregson said. "He was gone before we even got to the back door. You have no idea who he was?"

Mrs. Lynch shook her head.

"I didn't get a look at his face," she said. "He had a scarf wrapped around his nose and mouth. I was just so surprised to see him run through my house. What has become of this city?"

Gregson had heard the complaint before. Citizens clamoring for more police protection, but he knew budgets were being stretched as far as they could go without snapping. Still, it was difficult to defend a police department that had just spent a mint on a new police station with crime on the rise. Perhaps an increase in manpower would have been more prudent and once the crime rate fell then justify the cost of a new building. Nonetheless, it wasn't his decision to make or defend. He ignored her question as if it were rhetorical.

"Did you get a good look at his clothing?" Gregson asked.

Mrs. Lynch proceeded to describe the intruder to the best of her recollection. He didn't stand out in any fashion except for the scarf. The weather had grown warmer and the need for a scarf was unnecessary except if the man wanted to hide his identity.

"Is there anyone we can contact for you, Mrs. Lynch?" Gregson asked. "Someone to stay with you for a while? Maybe a relation of some kind?"

"My sister," she answered. "She lives with her husband a few blocks north of here."

Gregson took down the address and sent Hamm with the four-wheeler to fetch Mrs. Lynch's sister.

"Don't panic her," Watson cautioned Hamm. "She received a severe bump but it appears to be superficial at worst. She may experience a headache for a while but there should be no lasting effects. Let her sister know that immediately."

"Will do," Hamm said and left the scene.

"Is there anything we can do to make you more comfortable, Mrs. Lynch?" Gregson asked.

"You can catch the man who did this to me," she said not without a measure of acidity.

"We will do our best," Gregson said with all the sincerity he could muster. "If it's all right with you, Dr. Watson and I will return to Mr. Lestrade's rooms to make a search."

Mrs. Lynch nodded.

Dr. Watson gently patted her hand and followed the Inspector back up the stairs to Lestrade's rooms.

Chapter Twelve

In Lestrade's rooms, Gregson opened the drapes to let in as much light as possible.

"Obviously he didn't exit through the window, if Mrs. Lynch saw him run through her house," Dr. Watson said.

"Obviously," Gregson reiterated shutting the window that had been opened by the intruder.

"So where'd he hide while your back was turned?"

Gregson stepped over to a fairly large desk near the window but angled so the sunlight would fall on the desk and not the chair up against the wall behind it.

"Probably right here," Gregson said indicating the space between the desk and the chair. "This little spot can't be seen from this window. All the intruder had to do was squat down behind the desk while I was at the window and I'd never notice him. He really fooled me."

"It was classic misdirection. Like a magic trick."

"I thought I was too old to be fooled by magic tricks."

"Magic tricks, yes, but misdirection is something else entirely," Watson stated. "Holmes used to use misdirection on a number of occasions. I was nearly always taken off guard."

"Still," Gregson said but never finished. Instead he began a visual search of the room.

With the better lighting, Gregson could see there had been a somewhat systematic search of the room. A filing cabinet had been rifled with files strewn on the floor in an unorganized pile. Meanwhile, a small bookshelf had its contents removed and stacked carefully next to it. The cushions of a sofa had been removed and set against one wall while the sofa had been overturned to examine the bottom. The drawers of the desk used as a hiding place were emptied onto the desk, then discarded onto the floor and numerous papers and other items most often found in desk drawers were scattered across the desk top.

"This is a very strange mess," Watson stated looking around the room.

"You noticed that, too," Gregson said.

"It's like two people searched this room," Watson explained. "One who was systematic and another who didn't mind making a mess."

"Exactly," Gregson agreed.

"What do you make of that?" Watson asked.

"I think whoever coshed poor Mrs. Lynch arrived in these rooms first and was then frightened off by the second intruder, the one we chased, who then examined the room again. But as for which one did which search, I would only be able to guess."

"Not so," Watson said. "Look at the books stacked next to the bookshelf. See how they are piled upon a couple of pieces of paper which obviously came from the filing cabinet?"

"Yes," Gregson said with dawning reason. "You think the second intruder was the organized one because he piled the books neatly upon files already strewn about."

"Precisely," Watson said with a smile.

"So, what were they looking for?" Gregson asked examining the stack of books. "Was it the same thing or was each looking for something distinct?"

"I'm afraid my reasoning falls short when it comes to making that determination," Watson answered.

"Well, we've learned one thing," Gregson said removing two thin books from the stack on the floor and holding them up for Watson to examine.

"The Adventures of Sherlock Holmes," Watson said with more than a bit of pride. "Lestrade was an admirer?"

"Sure," Gregson said. "We all are down at the Yard. Maybe not enough to purchase two copies of the same book, like Lestrade obviously has done, but we read your stories when they appear in the Strand Magazine. That publication gets passed around the station until the pages are practically falling out."

Watson had never heard this, and he beamed with pride over the fact he was a celebrity among the ranks of London police officers.

"Well," Watson stated. "It's certain the intruders were not after copies of my work. Do you think they found what they were searching for?"

"If anything was discovered, it was only by the first one," Gregson said.

"Why would you say that?"

"If the second had discovered what he was searching for, he would have left prior to our arrival," Gregson said. "The fact he was still on the premises when we arrived makes me think he hadn't found what he was looking for."

"Sound thinking," Watson said. "I wish we knew what to look for."

Gregson shrugged his shoulders and began to look through the items on the desk. Meanwhile, Watson looked through the books including the double copies of "The Adventures of Sherlock Holmes."

"Why do you suppose Lestrade has two copies of this book?" Watson asked. "He doesn't have two copies of any other book."

The two books were contrary only in appearance; one was well read, the binding cracked, the pages dog eared, penciled notes written in the margins on a number of pages. The other was pristine as if it had recently been purchased but never been opened. Otherwise, they were the exact same book.

"Lestrade admired Mr. Holmes greatly," Gregson said. "I know he believed he could never be as intelligent as Mr. Holmes, but I also know he was striving to improve himself."

"Are you saying he was using this one as a sort of textbook?" Watson asked holding up the well-read book. He was also reminded of what Sgt. Rance had told him about studying the stories to improve himself.

"Perhaps," Gregson answered. "We won't know until we ask him. However, it's not like we at the Yard have the same privileges as Mr. Holmes."

"What privileges?"

"We get the cases assigned to us in the detective bureau," Gregson explained. "We don't get to pick and choose those that intrigue or challenge us. We're overworked and understaffed. We have to file reports. We have superiors to answer to. Mr. Holmes had none of that. So, if Lestrade wanted to study your friend's methods to make himself a better detective, I don't see any other way to do that than by reading and re-reading Mr. Holmes's cases."

"Then what's this one for?" Watson asked indicating the second volume.

Watson began flipping through the pages of the near perfect edition of "The Adventures" when a flimsy piece of paper worked itself free from the binding and fluttered to the floor.

"What's that?" Gregson asked pointing at the paper at

Watson's feet.

Watson bent over and retrieved the thin piece of paper.

"It's a telegram," he said upon identification.

"What's it say?" Gregson asked.

Watson unfolded it and read, "The man who can most help you is Ronald Adair STOP he is a member of the Bagatelle Card Club...oh my God."

Watson continued to stare at the telegram.

"What?" Gregson asked suddenly concerned at the look of shock on Watson's face. "What else does it say?"

"Nothing," Watson replied. "It's the signature."

Watson handed the telegram to Gregson who examined it and then looked back at Watson.

"H?" Gregson said.

"That's how Holmes would sign his telegrams," Watson said his voice a little uneven.

"Maybe it's an old telegram," Gregson said.

"Look at the date."

Gregson looked again at the telegram.

"Four days ago," he said.

"What do you think it means?" Watson asked.

"I don't know, but this can't be from Sherlock Holmes," Gregson said.

"Do you know anyone else named 'H' whom Lestrade was working with?"

"No one comes to mind," Gregson said thinking. "What if it does mean 'Holmes' but MYCROFT Holmes?"

"That would make sense," Watson said with relief.

"You appear relieved at that possibility," Gregson said.

"I am," Watson said. "For a moment I thought Sherlock

Holmes might still be alive somehow, although I don't know how. I saw his footprints and those of Professor Moriarty's go up to the edge of the falls. Neither returned. There was no other way out except down into the water. He can't have survived. If he had, surely he would have contacted me by now. It's been almost three years."

"Then it must be from Mycroft Holmes," Gregson said. "Which gives us another reason to visit him again. This time, we can bring along a piece of evidence."

Gregson held up the telegram.

"What about Ronald Adair?" Watson asked. "Does his name ring a bell?"

"No," Gregson said. "But I do know where the Bagatelle Card Club is."

Watson checks his watch.

"I think we should visit the Bagatelle Club first then return to the Diogenes Club." Watson offered. "Mycroft will have already had his dinner by the time we get there. I'd hate to interrupt that man while he was eating."

"Then that is what we'll do," Gregson agreed.

Watson and Gregson left Lestrade's rooms and returned to the sitting room downstairs.

Mrs. Lynch's sister, a near spitting image of Mrs. Lynch herself but slightly younger was already there comforting her sister while Hamm stood off to one side looking uncomfortable.

"Ah, Inspector," Hamm said upon spying his supervisor and eager to turn the matter over. "I brought Mrs. Lynch's sister just like you asked."

"Good work, Hamm," Gregson said then turned to Mrs. Lynch. "How are you feeling, Mrs. Lynch?"

"Much better, thank you, Inspector," she said. "May I introduce you to my sister Mrs. Eliza Winters."

Mrs. Winters nodded slightly.

"This is Inspector Gregson of Scotland Yard," Mrs. Lynch said and then proudly added, "and this is Dr. Watson of the Sherlock Holmes stories."

Mrs. Winters' eyes lit up at the mention of Dr. Watson's name.

"Indeed?" she said marveling at the celebrity in her midst. "This has been an exciting afternoon for you, Florence."

"It truly has," Mrs. Lynch said. "I have these three men to thank for securing my safety."

The three men mumbled some words of protest, but all three were enjoying the attention of being heroic in the eyes of these appreciative women.

"I'm afraid we have police matters to attend to, ladies," Gregson said. "I will send word to the Yard to have an extra patrol on your street for the next couple of days."

"Oh my," Mrs. Lynch said suddenly worried again. "Do you think the intruder will return?"

"I don't think so," Gregson said thinking nothing of the kind, but wanting to put the woman at ease. "Will your sister be able to stay with you for a while?"

"As long as she needs me," Mrs. Winters said. "And my husband will be along once he's finished with work."

"Wonderful," Gregson said. "Then we'll be off. Gentlemen?"

Inspector Gregson, Dr. Watson and Hamm all left the boarding house.

On the front sidewalk Gregson told Hamm of the plan for

the rest of the evening and all three piled into the four-wheeler and drove off toward the Bagatelle Club.

Chapter Thirteen

The four-wheeler pulled to a stop in front of the Bagatelle Card Club and Watson and Gregson disembarked.

"Head back to the Yard and set up that extra patrol for the ladies at Lestrade's boarding house, will you, Hamm?" Gregson said.

"Right, sir," Hamm said and drove off.

"As usual, I'll do the talking, but feel free to chime in should you feel the need," Gregson instructed once Hamm had driven away.

"I will," Watson agreed and the two mounted the short stairway up to the front door of the Bagatelle Club.

As they approached the door, it was suddenly opened and a man of military baring marched out past the doorman. He appeared taller than his actual average height due to the rigidity of his posture. He was thin but not weak looking and had muscular hands and forearms. His face was sun worn and leathery which could account for an older appearance than his true age.

"Have a good evening, Colonel Moran," the doorman said.

"Can't get much better than the night I just had at the tables, young man," the Colonel said with a smile and a tip of his hat to Watson and Gregson as they stood aside to allow him passage. "A wonderful night, indeed."

"I'm delighted to hear that, sir," the doorman said with a genuine smile as he accepted a small tip from the Colonel. "Thank you, sir."

The doorman was about to close the door when Gregson

grabbed it with his left hand.

"I'm sorry," the doorman said. "I don't recognize you as members. How can I help you?"

Gregson introduced himself and Dr. Watson and the doorman's face suddenly brightened.

"Ah, yes sirs, you are expected," he said and opened the door wider and invited them into the foyer.

"Just a moment," the doorman continued. "I'll make sure everything is ready."

The doorman walked off without another word.

"Expected?" Gregson queried.

"Strange," Watson said. "How could they possibly know we were coming?"

"I don't know."

"You're sure you've never heard of this Adair fellow?"

"Never," Gregson said. "What about you? Nothing from a past case?"

"Not that I can recall," Watson said.

A few moments later the doorman returned.

"Right this way, gentlemen," he said pleasantly and with a large almost whimsical smile.

He ushered Gregson and Watson past a large room where a number of men sat in groupings of four around a dozen or so tables where they all appeared to be engaged in card games. None seemed to take notice of the two men as they walked through the room and out another door opposite the main entrance. A short distance down one hallway and around a corner, Watson and Gregson were led to a small conference room.

The doorman knocked gently on the door and a quiet "come in" was the response from the interior.

The doorman opened the door and stood aside for Watson and Gregson to enter. Once they did, he quickly and quietly shut the door behind them.

The conference room had bookshelves lining three of the walls. The windows on the fourth wall were covered by heavy drapes that blocked all light from the outside. Gas lamps set on low barely illuminated the room and caused more of the outer perimeter to be shrouded in shadow than in any of the available light. However, the only brightly lit lamp was on a reading table where it was easily discernable that the man sitting there was not Ronald Adair, the club member they'd come to interrogate, but instead was the formidable Mycroft Holmes. He appeared very irritated and did not look happy in the least to be outside of his usual orbit.

"Well, well, Doctor Watson," Mycroft said in mock surprise. "I can honestly say I did not expect our paths to cross again so soon. And this must be the illustrious Inspector Tobias Gregson."

"I think I made myself perfectly clear upon our last meeting," Watson said anger rising like bile in his throat.

"You did, indeed," Mycroft said dismissively to Watson and turned his attention instantly to Gregson. "My brother spoke quite highly of you, Inspector."

"Thank you, sir?" Gregson said a little more questioningly than matter of fact.

"He said you were quite capable in your job and you did it well," Mycroft continued. "That's why I know you will believe me when I tell you some of my acquaintances have had a discussion with two or three of your superiors at the Yard about your recent investigation, and you are to cease any further inquiry. You will receive official orders upon your return to the Yard."

Gregson was stunned.

"As for you, Doctor," Mycroft continued. "I reiterate you have no idea what type of danger you have placed yourself in. You are not an official member of the Metropolitan Police Force and have no authority to investigate such matters nor do you have the protection that goes with being a member of the police."

"Your brother was not an officer, yet he still--"

"Damn it! My brother," Mycroft thundered, "was a 'consulting' detective. He did not initiate his investigations. Police and citizens came to him with problems. Who is your client? Whose interest do you represent?"

Watson stood silent.

"This is not meant to be a discussion," Mycroft said regaining most of his composure. "You are both being told to leave this matter alone. Have a pleasant evening."

As if on cue, the door to the conference room opened, and the doorman stood at attention to allow Watson and Gregson to exit.

They both walked out, and the doorman shut the door behind them leaving Mycroft Holmes alone.

Once he was certain Watson and Gregson could no longer be within earshot of the conference room, Mycroft cleared his throat.

The same shadowy figure Gregson had encountered at Lestrade's boarding house stepped into the dim lighting from a particularly darkened corner of the library.

"I gather you picked up on all of that?" Mycroft asked the stranger.

"Indeed. Especially your responses," the stranger said. "Do you think they'll listen this time?"

Mycroft let out a sigh as he pondered the question.

"Gregson will undoubtedly follow the orders of his superintendents," Mycroft said. "He understands his position and rank. But Watson...I don't know. You were correct in believing Watson would ignore my first warning and that he'd find the telegram to lead them here. It's unfortunate you were unable to locate it before their arrival."

"At least it didn't fall into the hands of the ruffian tasked with obtaining it," the figure stated.

"There is that bit of assurance," Mycroft said. "Unfortunately, I now fear an unnecessary window has been opened and may put a number of people in jeopardy."

"And Dr. Watson is at the forefront of that danger," the shadowy figure stated with concern. "Should he continue with his queries, sooner or later he will run afoul of one of our foes and possibly destroy years of investigation. I feel Watson will have to be monitored for his own safety. It may, in fact, be necessary to place him in some sort of protective custody."

"We can't put him in jail," Mycroft said. "The man's a writer. He'd have every newspaper in London screaming about his incarceration from their headlines.

"In a way," Mycroft continued. "I feel sorry for the Good Doctor. All he wants to do is make sure his friend is safe and everywhere he turns no one shows any interest in his cause. His recent loss has left him believing he is alone and, I'm afraid, nothing will sway him from his pursuits. There's only been one man Watson trusted implicitly and he's been dead for almost three years."

The shadowy figure thought for a moment.

"The time is drawing near for that to change," he said.

Chapter Fourteen

Dr. Watson and Inspector Gregson stood outside of the Bagatelle Card Club after basically having been "tossed" from the premises like a couple of interlopers.

"We are definitely out of our element on this investigation," Gregson said shaking his head.

"How can you say that?" Watson asked.

"Everyone knows of the pull Mr. Mycroft Holmes is capable of," Gregson said. "He holds a huge number of strings in his hand and he can tug on any one of them at any time and get things done. These aren't political favors, either. He controls a lot that goes on in this city. He can make things happen or make things cease to happen."

"So, you're actually going to drop this case," Watson said incredulously. "You're just going to leave your friend out there twisting in the wind, hurt, maybe even dead."

"It's not that I want to," Gregson said. "It's that I'll HAVE to. I'll get my orders when I return to headquarters. I won't have a choice.

"Besides, if Mycroft Holmes is truly involved," Gregson continued. "Then, with all he's capable of, could this investigation be in any better hands? Either way, I am sure I'm out of this one. My superiors will inform me along with the rest of the force that the search for Lestrade is being called off. Whether or not they deem it necessary to inform us of Her Majesty's Government taking over the investigation is another thing entirely."

Watson shook his head incredulously.

"We're definitely out of our element on this matter,"

Gregson repeated. "It hurts me to leave my friend's whereabouts unknown, but there is little I can do that wouldn't result in my dismissal. It's back to the Robbery Division for me."

"Well, I'm not giving up," Watson said quietly but firmly. "I must be on to something for Mycroft Holmes to deem it a priority to keep informing me I'm in grave danger."

Gregson nodded his head and looked back at the front facade of the Bagatelle Card Club and mumbled something Watson couldn't quite understand.

"What did you say?" Watson asked.

Gregson shook his head partially in disgust at his own actions and also in frustration.

"I said, 'How did he know?'" he answered.

"Know what?"

"How did Mycroft Holmes know we were coming here?"

"You're right," Watson said with some excitement. "He's very intelligent, even more so than his brother, but he couldn't possibly have known where we were going prior to us knowing it."

"Then it has to be the telegram," Gregson said. "It's the only clue we found and it's the reason that brought us here."

"He must be the one who sent it. The 'H' does stand for Holmes; Mycroft Holmes. He must have been working with Lestrade, after all. I'm positive he knows more than he's letting on."

"That was evident by this meeting."

"But do you think he might know where Lestrade is or, in the least, why he went missing?" Watson asked.

"Hmm," Gregson pondered. "I don't know. He might."

"I don't think he does," Watson said, "know where he is,

that is."

"Why not?"

"I don't know, actually. Just a feeling. Knowing what little I do know of him, I'd think he'd want to put us at ease if there were a plan afoot, and Lestrade was working with the government. He would never supply us with details, but he'd try to reassure us all was well in hand. I think I should take some time to think about matters."

"I think you should," Gregson said with concern. "It's easier for me to let this go if I have a supervisor ordering me to do so. I can see the dilemma you're in."

"Dinner Friday night?" Watson asked suddenly changing the subject.

"That sounds wonderful," Gregson agreed. "We can bring each other up to date on... anything."

"Friday night, then, at the Criterion at six," Watson said and stuck his arm up to hail a passing hansom.

The cab pulled to the curb and Watson climbed in without another word to Gregson.

Gregson heard Watson give his address to the driver and the cab pulled from the curb and traveled down the street.

Chapter Fifteen

Watson had to do some thinking. The cabby dropped him at his home just as the gas lamps were being lit on his street. It wasn't until Watson had entered his home that he suddenly realized just how exhausted he truly was. The day had been an extremely taxing one and he wanted nothing more than a good night's sleep but he knew there were things he had to contemplate before he could rest. So, Watson prepared himself a light meal of bread and cheese and sat down to eat it. He poured himself a half glass of wine at the end of his meal and retired to the comfort of his sitting room where he could contemplate the events of the day and mull over the many questions he had regarding Lestrade's disappearance and his subsequent investigation.

What exactly did Mycroft Holmes know about the disappearance of Inspector Lestrade and why was he keeping it all a secret only to himself? Why did Mycroft keep telling him he was in danger? What danger? How did Mycroft know he and Gregson would be at the Bagatelle Card Club? Was it because of the telegram he'd found or was there some other solution? Was Mycroft the mastermind behind Lestrade's disappearance and if so what was the motive in snatching him?

Mycroft knew of Watson's discretion if for no other reason than for the case involving the King of Bohemia where Watson held back telling the tale for two years based on the instruction from the royal personage himself. (17) Watson could easily be trusted with any information that Lestrade was safe and sound and working on something for the British Government if that were the case. There was no need for all of the cloak and dagger, penny dreadful, mysterious meetings between them.

Watson had been a great friend to Mycroft's brother, Sherlock. Surely, Mycroft was aware of that fact. If he were so damned intelligent, he would know Watson's silence was easily procured especially in matters of national security.

"That can't be the case," Watson thought. "Mycroft must not know of Lestrade's whereabouts because he'd certainly put my mind at ease if he were safe. It also wouldn't be prudent to continue to allow Scotland Yard to keep wasting resources in a vain search for the Inspector."

There had to be something else.

These questions had to point to one solution. But what? Watson felt as though his mind were in an impenetrable fog.

Lestrade was working on something involving this Adair fellow and it was Mycroft who had put him on the scent. There was no one else already involved in this case with an "H" initial. But this was flimsy evidence and Watson knew it. Truly the "H" could be anyone, possibly even the person responsible for Lestrade's abduction.

What if this line of thinking were in error?

What if the shadowy figure Gregson had encountered were searching for anything that could tell him what Lestrade was investigating? Perhaps the shadow is the person responsible for Lestrade's kidnapping and he isn't getting anywhere with Lestrade. Lestrade won't talk so the shadow searches his rooms.

But that doesn't explain the fact that at least two people searched those rooms and one of them was responsible for clocking Mrs. Lynch on the head in order to access the rooms. Since the shadowy subject was the last in the rooms before Watson and Gregson arrived, it stood to reason he was the one who made Mrs. Lynch comfortable and removed her kettle from the stove burner and probably frightened off the original intruder. However, there were other matters, of a more personal nature, that nagged at Watson.

Why had Holmes told him their old rooms in Baker Street had been set ablaze when they obviously hadn't been? Mrs. Hudson, herself, had verified that fact. Was it to keep Watson away from 221B for some reason? If so, what? Why was Mycroft Holmes paying to continue the rent on the old rooms? What plans did he have for them? Certainly it wasn't out of the goodness of his heart for Mrs. Hudson's well-being and judging by her claims of self-sufficiency the money wasn't even needed. There was also Lestrade's recent upturn in successfully closing out cases. Could he have actually done that all on his own, or was he actually getting assistance from someone? And finally that telegram. That damned telegram! The "H" signature. It bothered Watson more than anything. It had to have been sent by Mycroft Holmes, but...

Could it be? Watson thought.

Could it be that Sherlock Holmes was...somehow...still alive?

It would fit the facts and answer the questions about Baker Street and Lestrade's success rate, but then where had he been for the last three years and how had he avoided death? And more importantly, why had he not made contact?

"When you have eliminated the impossible," Watson heard his old friend's voice in his head talking to him. "Whatever remains, no matter how improbable, must be the truth."

But Holmes WAS dead.

It was IMPOSSIBLE for him not to be.

That had to be eliminated.

Sherlock Holmes could not possibly be alive. Therefore, he did not send the telegram found in Lestrade's rooms or assist Lestrade in any of his recent cases.

The wine began to work and Watson relaxed to the point of actually falling asleep in his easy chair once again.

It wasn't greatly comfortable but neither was the bed without Mary.

Watson let sleep envelop him.

Chapter Sixteen

The morning sun streaming through Dr. Watson's front window woke him long before his first appointment was due to arrive. Watson attempted to work the stiffness out of his spine from his second night of sleep in the easy chair and did his best to refresh himself with a quick wash and a shave. He felt better after the wash, but the stiffness remained.

The late morning and early afternoon passed quickly due to an influx of new patients with barely a moment for reflection on the Lestrade matter, but once dinner time approached and the appointments ended, Watson found himself thinking again about his missing friend and the supposed danger he was in. Danger they both were in.

He had received no threats except for those from Mycroft Holmes, and they were veiled at best. Gregson was being intimidated into dropping the investigation, but that seemed to be more politically motivated than nefarious in nature.

Watson's stomach made an embarrassing growling noise and for the first time in a few weeks he actually felt hungry and not just the necessity to eat. He retrieved his hat and coat from the rack and left the house walking along his street until he found an available hansom and flagged it down.

"Can you recommend a good restaurant in the area?" Watson asked the driver.

"Goldini's on Gloucester's supposed to have good food," the driver said in a gravelly voice slightly muffled by the scarf around his face. "Never been meself, though, guv'nor."

"That sounds fine," Watson said climbing into the cab.

The cab took Watson to the restaurant which seemed a

greater distance than he'd expected, but he wasn't disappointed once the food arrived at his table.

There was nothing fancy about the fare. Watson dined on simple, yet delicious, steak and kidney pie with a small endive salad and a large slice of chocolate cake for dessert. It was absolutely delightful and quite filling. It was a mundane, simple pleasure; a momentary return to everyday life.

Upon his return to his home, Watson discovered he had neglected the collection of his mail for the entire day. He removed a number of envelopes from his mailbox and flipped through them. There seemed to be nothing important within the post except for a single, small, plain envelope with the name "Dr. Watson" scrawled upon it. No address. No return address. No postmark. It must have been hand delivered outside of the postal service.

Watson opened the plain envelop and discovered a page torn from a newspaper. One side had advertisements for hair tonics and shaving utensils but the other was a series of personal ads with one circled blatantly in red ink.

It read: "R.A. - They are on his trail and want to flush him out. Keep your eye on the Colonel. - G.L."

Hand printed along the side margin in the same red ink were scrawled the words "The game is afoot."

Watson's face flushed with anger.

Who would do such a cruel thing? He wondered.

To create a note that so blatantly appeared to be the work of his old friend was unconscionable.

Watson crumpled the note and envelope and jammed them into his trouser pocket where he also reached for the house key that dangled from a chain attached to a pen knife given to him by his late wife. He located the house key among some others and forcefully stuck it into the lock and turned it. Tearing the key from the keyhole, Watson wrenched open the door and was about to enter, when he was stopped by a strange sound from the street.

A whispering noise followed instantly by a soft whistling as something flashed passed the side of his face and impacted on the wall next to his door and just above the nameplate that identified his profession.

In a split second Watson's hand flexed to grasp his mail and keys in his fist. He turned his head toward the sound of impact on his house. There he spotted what appeared to be a bullet hole. He raced into his home and slammed the door shut as he entered.

Watson dashed to his desk in his sitting room. He scattered his mail on the floor then wrestled with the knife and keys he still held in his hand until he located the one for his desk. He fumbled to open the desk drawer but when he finally got it open he pulled it nearly completely from the desk. The only items contained in this drawer were his loaded service revolver and additional ammunition.

Watson grabbed the revolver taking only a moment to glance at the photograph of his beautiful wife, and ran to the front door where he opened it and stormed outside ready to take on whoever it was who had just tried to kill him.

"Show yourself!" Watson hollered at the top of his lungs. His anger overpowering his decorum.

The few people who were on the street heard Watson's angry cry and panicked when they saw him waving about a pistol. They ran for cover anywhere they could find it. There were a couple of startled screams from some of the women in the vicinity. The slight carriage traffic halted. One carriage was brought to such a severe stop, the horse reared up on its hind legs in protest. Some drivers tried to turn their carriages to head in an opposing direction but found themselves with unwilling or confused horses.

A lone Bobby saw and heard the commotion and pulled his whistle from the pocket on his uniform and blew it three times in rapid succession. Then slowly crossed the street to confront Dr. Watson.

"Are you all right, sir?" the constable asked and then recognized who the man with the revolver was. "Dr. Watson?"

Overcome with rage, Watson gave only a passing glance at the officer and then began looking around the street again.

"You coward!" he called to the street. "Snipe at me will you? Come out and fight me fairly!"

"Dr. Watson," the officer said again, this time with a bit more force but also with an obvious amount of compassion. Around a corner came two more officers running at top speed, but the constable gestured for them to slow down and approach with care. They stopped running but continued to close in on Dr. Watson.

"Dr. Watson," the constable said again, this time gaining Watson's attention.

"Evert?" Watson said upon recognizing the young patrolman and his rage immediately began to recede. "Is it you?"

"Yes, Doctor," Evert said compassionately as the other two constables neared the scene. "What's happened here? Why are you waving a gun about?"

"Someone shot at me," Watson said.

"Shot at you?" Evert said with surprise. "I heard no shot, Doctor."

"I'm not imagining things, Evert!" Watson thundered.

"I'm not saying you are, Doctor. Just tell me what happened."

"I had just retrieved my mail…" Watson began.

"How about you lower the pistol first, Doctor," Evert said as he was joined by the other officers.

Watson looked at the revolver in his hand and saw it was inadvertently pointed in Evert's general direction. He immediately lowered it, then took his finger off the trigger, turned the gun around and handed it to Evert.

"Let's take this off the street," Evert said taking the weapon and then motioning toward Dr. Watson's door.

Watson nodded and walked back inside his home with Evert behind him.

"I'll be all right," Evert told the other two officers. "Go ahead and restore order to the street."

The other two officers nodded and each took a side of the street to let the pedestrians know all was well.

Evert entered Watson's home and closed the front door behind him. Watson was already seated in his easy chair, a glass of whiskey on the side table next to him. His hands were shaking but whether that was due to fear or anger, Evert didn't know.

"All right, Doctor," Evert said placing the revolver on Watson's desk and taking a seat opposite him in the other armchair. "Tell me what happened."

Watson told the young constable what had occurred only a few minutes prior.

"I swear to you, Doctor," Evert said. "I heard no shot. I

155

was just down the street from you."

"It was somehow suppressed," Watson said his voice much more subdued than that of a few minutes before. "I heard what sounded like a puff of air. Something whizzed past my head and struck the wall next to my front door. I'm not imagining this and I'm not making it up. Go look for yourself."

Evert got up from his chair and went back outside to examine the wall next to Dr. Watson's front door.

Just above the nameplate proclaiming the premises to be Dr. Watson's office was a hole and judging from the freshness of the chipped brick, it was recently made.

Using a penknife, Evert dug into the hole and came up with a snub nosed bullet.

Evert examined the bullet as closely as he could from the street. He was still peering at it when one of the two Bobbies returned.

"Everything all right, Evert?" the bobby asked.

"Yes," Evert said spying his fellow officer. "You got everyone calmed down?"

"Yeah," the constable said. "Weren't no easy trip neither. Seein' a man standing on his stoop wavin' a gun about. Bound to scare the skin off most people. You gonna bring him in?"

"No," Evert said.

"Why not? Disturbin' the peace in the very least, he was, actin' that way."

"It's more like self-defense," Evert argued and produced the bullet for the bobby to see.

"Blimey," the constable said a little surprised. "Bloke was tellin' the truth."

"He was," Evert said. "Do me a favor and summon

Inspector Gregson from the Yard, will you?"

"Right-o," the constable said then looked around at the buildings on the street. "You gonna be all right here? What if'n someone takes another shot?"

"I'll be fine. I'll wait inside. Just get Inspector Gregson. Thank you."

The constable nodded and dashed off to summon the inspector.

Evert went back into Dr. Watson's house.

"What was that all about?" Watson asked. "You were gone for quite a while."

"I was retrieving evidence," Evert said and showed Dr. Watson the bullet.

"You see," Watson said his agitation returning. "I told you. I wasn't lying."

"I didn't think you were, Doctor," Evert said. "I've called for Inspector Gregson."

"I don't think he's going to be able to help."

"Why not?"

"He and I have been ordered to keep our noses out of the Lestrade business."

"You're not the only ones," Evert stated.

"What do you mean?" Watson asked.

"The whole force," Evert said. "We've all been told to stop looking; that the matter is being handled by a higher authority...government, I guess."

"So, no one in Scotland Yard is looking for the Inspector?"

Evert shook his head.

"Damn them," Watson said. "Damn them to hell!"

"Please, Doctor. Don't upset yourself," Evert said.

"How can you sit there and tell me that?" Watson asked incredulously. "Did you know Inspector Lestrade? Were you acquainted with him at all?"

"Of course, Doctor," Evert said with sympathy. "There isn't a man on the force who isn't upset and concerned by this. We want to be out on the streets looking for the Inspector, too. Do you think this has something to do with his disappearance?"

"It has to," Watson said slightly calmer. "What else could it be?"

"I don't know."

"Who told you not to continue searching for the Inspector?"

"Our sergeant, at the daily brief," Evert said. "All shifts are getting the same notice. He said it comes from the highest ranks, but he has no other information other than someone higher in rank is handling the investigation now."

"Then Lestrade must have been involved in something big," Watson said sitting back in his chair to think.

The two men sat silently for a few minutes before there came the sound of a carriage clattering to a stop in front of Watson's home.

Evert jumped from his chair and ran to the front door. Watson grabbed up his revolver from his desk and readied himself for another threat.

Chapter Seventeen

Evert opened the front door, his truncheon in his hand but hidden behind the door, to discover Inspector Gregson disembarking from the police carriage parked in front of Dr. Watson's home.

"Is he all right?" Gregson said climbing the few steps to Watson's door. "Is Doctor Watson all right?"

"He's fine, sir," Evert said and saw Gregson relax. "I've been sitting with him."

"Thank God," Gregson gasped.

Evert pointed out the pock mark on the exterior wall just above Dr. Watson's nameplate. Gregson nodded then entered Watson's home.

When Watson spotted Gregson enter through the front door, he immediately returned the revolver to his desk, and Evert returned his truncheon to his belt then shut the door.

"Inspector," Watson said with as much calm as possible. "You've heard what happened?"

"Just a bit, Doctor," Gregson said and entered the sitting room followed by Evert who stood at attention in the doorway. "You were shot at?"

"Yes," Watson said.

Evert presented Gregson with the snub-nosed revolver bullet who took it and gave it a cursory examination.

"The evidence bears that out," Gregson said tucking the bullet into his vest pocket.

Gregson took a seat in the guest's armchair while Watson resumed his seat in the opposite chair.

"Do you feel up to telling me what happened as best you

can remember it?" Gregson asked removing his notebook and pencil from his pocket.

For the second time, Watson related his tale.

Gregson looked puzzled after Watson ended his narrative.

"You've thought of something?" Watson asked. "I can see it on your face."

"You said you were looking through your mail for two or three minutes," Gregson confirmed.

"Closer to two, I'd think," Watson said.

"And nothing happened until you were attempting to enter your home?"

"Correct."

"Why do you suppose the gunman would wait until you were moving before taking the shot? You were standing still, while you were looking through your mail, weren't you?"

"I was," Watson said understanding where the Inspector was going with his queries. "But you raise a good point. Why not take the shot at a stationary target? Why wait until I had the door open and easy access to cover before shooting at me?"

Gregson pondered this for a moment.

"Maybe the shot was just a warning?" Evert said more as a question than a statement of fact.

"Precisely," Gregson said. "It's what I was thinking."

"Because of the Lestrade matter?" Watson asked.

"Possibly," Gregson said. "Unless you can think of some other reason?"

"I can't," Watson said.

Gregson sighed.

"Well," he said. "Now I don't see that Mr. Mycroft Holmes can keep me out of this. Not when one of Her Majesty's subjects has had an attempt made upon his life in the streets of London."

"Perhaps another visit to the Diogenes Club would be in order," Watson said.

"Perhaps," Gregson said still thinking. "You have no idea where the shot came from?"

"None," Watson said. "I was facing the front of my building. Somewhere in the street or from a building across the street. I don't really know."

Gregson rose from his chair and walked to the front door.

"Please, follow me, Doctor," the inspector said as he left the sitting room.

Doctor Watson and Constable Evert followed the Inspector back outside to the front stoop of the building. Gregson again examined the bullet hole in the brick near Dr. Watson's nameplate.

"And you're certain you heard no shot?" Gregson asked Watson and readied his pencil as if to jot down Watson's response.

"None," Watson said. "Just a puff of air."

Instead of writing down Watson's answer, Gregson took his pencil and inserted it into the hole in the brick outside Watson's residence. It fit snugly but when he released it he was able to determine the trajectory of the bullet as the pencil pointed in a downward direction toward the street.

"That's amazing, Inspector," Watson said marveling at the detective's ingenuity.

"Not really," Gregson replied. "I learned it from...a mutual friend."

"What does it tell you?" Evert asked looking closely at

the pencil.

"Just the direction from which the shot came," Gregson replied and pointed out the trajectory indicated by the slant of the pencil for Evert to follow. "It looks like the bullet was fired from just across the street on a slight angle away from your doorstep, Doctor."

"And it had to be at close range for you to hear a silenced weapon," Evert added.

"Do you remember anyone in that area when you got to your front door?" Gregson asked.

"No," Watson said shaking his head. "I'm afraid not. I wasn't really paying any attention to my surroundings. I recall the street seemed strangely busy; more pedestrians than usual but no one who stood out."

"What about you, Evert?" Gregson asked the young officer.

"Me, sir?" he asked surprised.

"Yes. Do you recall anyone out of the ordinary along your beat prior to the commotion?"

"No one," Evert said. "It had been a quiet shift until...well... Dr. Watson's outburst."

"I had just been fired upon, young man," Watson said taking offense. "I'd like to know what you would have done in the same circumstances."

"I...I didn't mean to insult you, Doctor," Evert stammered. "I was just stating the facts as I was aware of them at the time. I didn't even recognize you at that moment. All I saw was a man waving a revolver and threatening the street."

"Maybe we should take this conversation back indoors," Gregson suggested.

Watson nodded and led the way back into his home followed by the two police officers.

Chapter Eighteen

Dr. Watson offered the two armchairs to Gregson and Evert and took a seat behind his desk. He removed his revolver from the desk top and put it into its usual drawer where he used his keys to lock and secure it. His hands were shaking slightly, partly from fear at being shot at but mostly due to the fact the rush of adrenalin that so recently coursed through his body was beginning to subside. However, the anger at the attempt was still fresh and bubbling beneath the surface of his barely composed exterior.

"Would either of you care for a drink?" Watson asked but didn't make an attempt to go to the sideboard where he kept his glasses and decanter.

Both officers declined.

"I am at a loss," Watson said. "I have no idea of what to do next."

"Your safety should be of the first priority," Gregson suggested.

"Agreed," Evert said.

"What do you recommend?" Watson asked.

"Perhaps you should take a holiday," Gregson offered. "Leave the city for a few days. Maybe a week."

"And do what?" Watson asked. "Sit by the seaside? Tour the country?"

"What about..." Evert started.

After a moment's hesitation, Watson said, "Go on."

"What about going somewhere quiet and doing some...writing," Evert expounded. "You could work on some more of the stories of the cases you handled with Mr. Holmes that haven't already been published. I'm sure people would enjoy reading them."

"Lestrade made the same suggestion the last time we were together."

"Then it must be a good idea," Evert said with a smile. "Don't you think?"

"I don't know if I'm ready for that yet," Watson said sadly.

"Doctor," Gregson responded compassionately. "I don't mean to sound insulting, but it's been three years now. How long before you ARE ready?"

Watson shook his head.

"You know the public would relish a new adventure or two and it might help for you to relive some good memories."

"You may be right," Watson brightened slightly.

There was a sudden knocking at Watson's front door, more like a pounding.

"Want me to see to that?" Evert asked the Inspector.

"We'll both go," Gregson said. "Doctor, stay here."

Watson remained at his desk but unlocked the desk drawer and removed the revolver. He kept it in his hand on his lap but concealed by the desk. He noticed Evert remove his truncheon from the loop on his belt and hold it at the ready.

"Who is it?" Gregson stated in an authoritative tone.

"It's Mr. Mycroft Holmes come to speak with Dr. Watson," came the voice of the Great Detective's brother in response. It was just as authoritative as Gregson's if not more so.

Gregson opened the door and Mycroft Holmes entered without invitation. His large size practically forcing Gregson and Evert out of the way. Outside at the curb sat Mycroft's four-wheeler and bundled driver who maintained the reins of the horse. Gregson noticed his own carriage had been forced forward to allow Mycroft's to be perpendicular with the front door of Dr. Watson's home.

"Dr. Watson," Mycroft said ignoring the police officers and walking into the sitting room. "I have seen more physical activity in the last few days than I have in the last few years. I'll give you one guess as to why that is."

Watson didn't reply.

"It's because of you," Mycroft continued.

Watson removed his revolver from beneath the desk and placed it on the desk top.

"Threats will get you nowhere, Doctor," Mycroft said dismissively glancing at the gun.

"I'm not threatening you, Mr. Holmes," Watson said his voice showing remarkable restraint for the anger he felt. "But if the need to do so becomes necessary...well..."

Watson glanced at the loaded pistol on his desk.

Mycroft Holmes drew in and released a great breath.

"Inspector Gregson," Mycroft said keeping his gaze on Watson. "You and your assistant are dismissed."

"Sir," Gregson said. "I'm investigating an attempt on Dr. Watson's life, I've …"

"I'm well aware of your investigation," Mycroft interrupted, looking sternly at Gregson. "Take it from me, you're investigation is over. It is now being handled by the highest level of Her Majesty's Service."

"Again?" Gregson said angrily. "Do I even have a job at the Yard anymore or is this 'highest level' going to be handling ALL of my assignments?"

"Your tone is not appreciated, Inspector," Mycroft said.

"I don't care. A devoted servant of the Crown just had an attempt made on his life. If that isn't something for the Yard to be investigating, I don't know what we should be doing."

"Just do what you're told," Mycroft said, "and all will be well. You need to let this matter alone."

"But Dr. Watson's safety," Gregson argued.

"Will be maintained as long as he cooperates," Mycroft said and turned back to face Dr. Watson. "Now, if you don't mind, the Doctor and I have important matters to discuss and they do not include members of Scotland Yard."

Gregson looked past the immense figure of Mycroft Holmes and toward Dr. Watson.

"Doctor," he said. "I will be only a telegram's distance away, if you should need me."

"Thank you, Inspector," Watson said.

"Come along, Evert," Gregson said and the two police officers left Dr. Watson's house.

Chapter Nineteen

Once the police officers had left his home, Watson stared at Mycroft and refused to offer him a chair or a libation. He didn't feel he'd be able to intimidate the great man in any significant manner, but he wanted Mycroft to know he'd have no chance at intimidation on his end either.

"How did you know about the attempt on my life?" Watson asked Mycroft suspiciously.

"It is my business to know what other people don't know," Mycroft said. "I'm sure that is a phrase you've heard uttered before." **(18)**

"Your brother often said it to his clients," Watson replied. "I think I may have mentioned it in the Blue Carbuncle matter."

"You did," Mycroft said.

Watson suddenly realized Mycroft had read his published accounts of his brother's exploits. Was it possible he was an admirer of the adventures? Watson was eager to know, but didn't want to give Mycroft the possibility of denigrating his writing.

"Still doesn't answer my question though, does it?" Watson asked more as a statement than a question.

"Doctor, I have little time for these games," Mycroft argued. "You have jeopardized a major investigation – one that may very well have the outcome of war or peace."

Watson's eyes widened slightly at the mention of war.

"Furthermore," Mycroft said with the attitude of a teacher over an exceptionally dim student. "You realize the consequences of your actions, and you do nothing to change them."

"I realize I am about to lose another friend," Watson said

sternly. "I will not be talked to like a child; not in my own home. I don't give a damn about your 'major investigation.' I don't appreciate secrets being kept from me. I took a bullet while in Her Majesty's service. As an Army surgeon, I watched men lose limbs, lives and hope. All while the politicians and strategists talked and planned and made decisions completely ignorant to what was truly occurring in the trenches."

"Are you finished?" Mycroft asked sarcastically.

"I haven't even started," Watson responded with a sarcastic laugh of his own. "You had every opportunity to assist me or ask for my assistance, yet you did nothing but flaunt your authority in my face as if I were some underling of yours. Like I was no more important to you than the man who drives your carriage."

"Now," Watson continued. "It seems, I've made some sort of progress in my efforts or someone wouldn't be shooting at me. Since, I've undoubtedly stepped on the right toes, I have no intention of halting my investigation. You will have to put me under arrest to stop me, and if that occurs, you and anyone else involved in this case can expect to read about it in the free press."

Watson crossed his arms in satisfaction.

"Now," Watson said. "Do YOU finally realize the consequences of YOUR actions?"

Mycroft Holmes drew in and released a great sigh and just stared at Dr. Watson.

"Nothing? Then you can march yourself out of my home," Watson said. "And you can expect a bill for a consultation fee since you've taken up time in my office."

Watson then moved his hand closer to the revolver.

"You don't want to do that, Doctor," Mycroft said with

just a hint of apprehension in his voice.

"I'm starting to think I do," Watson countered. "You have blocked me at every turn. Now, you come in here claiming to have information about the attempt on my life but unwilling to share any of it. I think I'm looking at the person responsible for that attempt or, in the very least, the one who ordered it."

"I did no such thing, Dr. Watson," Mycroft said and indicated an easy chair.

Watson nodded and Mycroft took a seat.

"We've been keeping an eye on you, Doctor," Mycroft continued.

"Who's 'we?'" Watson asked.

"The Diogenes Club," Mycroft said. "By now, I'm sure you've discovered the "Club for the most unclubbable men" is just a front for Her Majesty's Secret Service."

Watson had discovered no such thing, but he wasn't about to give Mycroft the upper hand when it came to disclosing information. He allowed Mycroft to believe what he wanted.

Mycroft then made the decision to take a more compassionate tact in his confrontation with the Good Doctor. He sat silently for a few contemplative moments until he saw Watson relax the hand nearest the service revolver.

"Doctor," Mycroft said in a much more easy tone. "You're absolutely correct."

Mycroft smiled agreeably and this gave Watson the impression it was not an often used expression.

"You have been treated shabbily," Mycroft continued. "But you must understand my position."

Mycroft paused for a response from Watson, but none was forthcoming.

"What I am about to tell you can go no further that this room," Mycroft said. "Am I understood?"

Watson nodded but didn't feel it necessary to respond verbally. He could discern the silence was encouraging his guest to speak more freely.

"Did my brother ever give you details into what Moriarty and his army of criminals were planning?" Mycroft asked.

"Not much," Watson said. "Only that Moriarty was running a large criminal empire here in London. He said Moriarty was responsible for half that is evil and nearly all that is undetected. He called him the Napoleon of Crime." **(19)**

"He was far worse than that," Mycroft stated. "His plans were far-reaching."

"How far?" Watson asked.

"All of England as well as the United States of America," Mycroft stated to Watson's shock. "In fact, it is said in hushed criminal circles, that he wanted the whole world and was working on succeeding in that endeavor."

"How could that even be possible?"

"If someone can apply the proper influences against the correct people, he can accomplish quite a bit," Mycroft answered cryptically but with the belief Watson would know his meaning.

"You're talking about blackmail?" Watson asked. "Blackmail of politicians and world leaders?"

"Only as the financial portion of the Professor's plan, yes," Mycroft said.

"Only a portion?" Watson verified. "What else was Moriarty devising?"

"According to Sherlock's clandestine investigations," Mycroft explained. "Moriarty was planning a military takeover of the United States."

"Impossible," Watson blurted and laughed. "How could he mount such an endeavor without an army or the funds in which to purchase even enough mercenaries?"

"That's where the plan begins," Mycroft said. "His blackmail dealings were bringing in thousands and he was recruiting criminals from both sides of the Pond to organize into armies. The Colonies beat us in their war for independence by utilizing soldiers who dressed without uniforms and engaged in renegade combat. England had a superior force in the late eighteenth century but we were no match for soldiers who fought from hiding places and retreated to unpopulated areas to regroup.

"We were truly unable to control the new nation," Mycroft continued. "When they got assistance from France and Spain, we knew we'd never win. England was able to hold a few large cities but never for long and our grasp kept releasing other portions of the Colonies while we held them."

"What has this to do with Moriarty's plan?" Watson asked.

"Moriarty saw an opportunity due to America's weakened state from the Civil War," Mycroft explained. "He had been in contact with a number of British military men, many retired but willing to join his ranks, who agreed with his appraisal for striking at a weakened America and returning her to British rule."

"Do you take me for a fool? This is outrageous!" Watson exclaimed obviously upset at the possibility the army he had served and taken a wound for could even remotely be involved in such a plot.

"It was our original assumption as well," Mycroft said in a calm voice that brought Watson's ire down. "However, my brother discovered evidence to the contrary.

"Through a mole he had operating within Moriarty's gang," Mycroft continued. "He was able to ferret out the information needed to launch the investigation and name a few names. The men still in the military were quietly removed from service and those who had resigned their commissions were removed...as well."

"What does that mean?" Watson asked.

Mycroft simply stared at Watson and raised an eyebrow.

"I see," Watson said as a dark dawning came to him. "Can you tell me...was anyone from the Fifth Northumberland Fusiliers, my old regiment, involved?"

"None," Mycroft said with another uncomfortable but reassuring smile.

Watson let out a sigh of relief.

"What happened next proceeded very quickly," Mycroft said. "Sherlock and nearly a platoon of Scotland Yarders tracked and arrested over a hundred members of Moriarty's gang. But as you are aware, Moriarty and a few of his closest henchmen were able to escape. One of those we are still pursuing is Colonel Sebastian Moran."

Watson's eyes widened.

"You've heard of him?" Mycroft asked surprised.

"A Colonel Moran was at the Bagatelle Club," Watson said. "He was leaving as we arrived."

"That is one of the four clubs where he has membership," Mycroft said. "He is at the top of our most watched list, but there is a slipperiness to him. He can often escape our nets when it suits him."

"I see," Watson said.

"As I was saying," Mycroft continued. "We contacted the Marshal's Service in the United States and informed them of the plot and they simultaneously held raids that apprehended dozens more military personnel in the U.S. (20) In conjunction with the "Private Eyes" in the Pinkerton Detective Agency, this was also done swiftly and with little public notice."

"You're telling me," Watson said with more than a note of incredulity in his tone. "That Great Britain and the United States of America were poised for another war but a handful of Scotland Yarders and...what do you call those Pinkerton fellows?"

"Private Eyes," Mycroft offered. (21)

"Yes, Private Eyes, were responsible for foiling the entire plot?"

"That is exactly what I'm telling you, Doctor Watson," Mycroft said and his tone had grown suddenly more serious and cold than Watson had ever heard it.

"How is it Gregson knows nothing of this?"

"Because my brother did not trust him," Mycroft said.

"Didn't trust him?" Watson asked shocked. "How could he not? They'd worked together. Holmes knew of his dedication to the police force."

"He trusted Lestrade to a much higher level and there was rumor that some of the Yard might be involved in the plot," Mycroft said. "That proved later to be only a rumor but at the time, my brother was playing it safe.

"He and Lestrade put together the team that brought down the Moriarty gang," Mycroft continued. "Even at that, most of the men involved simply thought they were breaking up an enormous crime ring. They weren't aware of the true plans of the gang and the members of our own military."

"But why didn't Holmes tell me?" Watson asked emotion leaking into his voice. "Surely, I was trustworthy. Surely, he could count on me to be at his side in such an important case."

"Of course, he could," Mycroft said reassuringly. "He also knew you were newly married and he didn't want to jeopardize your wife or your safety."

Watson nodded but this was not quite making sense for him.

He drew in a deep breath and asked, "So what happens now?"

"Now," Mycroft said. "We put you into protective custody."

"What?" Watson asked shocked. "That's out of the question. I have patients relying on me."

"You should have thought of them before you went against my warnings," Mycroft said with a slight smile of triumph. "Now, with this recent attempt on your life, my office has no choice but to take you out of circulation, so to speak, until the entire matter is resolved. It's for your own safety and that of your patients. Can't have them showing up if you have bullets flying about."

"Where am I to go?" Watson asked. "What will I be doing?"

"We already have a room for you at the Northumberland Hotel," Mycroft said. "You'll be very comfortable. You may do whatever you wish as long as you do it within the confines of your rooms at the hotel. Read. Write. Enjoy fine meals and good wine all at Her Majesty's expense."

"I'd feel as though I were taking advantage," Watson countered.

"Think of it as payment for a long overdue debt."

"What debt?"

"For your wound in battle and for your services alongside my brother," Mycroft said. "He became a better man for knowing you, Dr. John Watson."

This last statement touched Watson deeply and for the first time in a very long time, it seemed, he felt a great deal of self-worth.

"All right, Mr. Holmes," Watson said. "I'll go to the hotel. Thank you for bringing me in to your confidence."

Mycroft nodded in agreement and then struggled to free himself from his armchair.

"What will I need to bring with me?" Watson asked.

"A number of changes of clothing and whatever materials, books or writing implements, you see fit to occupy your time while you're in our...care," Mycroft instructed.

"You mean 'custody', don't you?"

"Look upon it how you will," Mycroft said with a dismissive wave of his hand. "You'll be treated better than anyone else my office ever had in its...care."

"Will there be a guard?"

"Do I need to post one?"

"No," Watson said.

"Then there won't be one," Mycroft said. "Besides, it would draw attention to your stay."

"So I'd be free to leave?"

"I wouldn't recommend it," Mycroft warned. "You seem to be a marked man now, Doctor. It would be best for you to stay in your suite and enjoy your holiday."

"It'll take me a few minutes to pack a bag," Watson said.

"Will I be going with you or will you send another carriage?"

"I believe we can take you, Doctor," Mycroft agreed. "Provided you make haste...and you'll need to leave...that...behind."

Mycroft indicated the revolver on Watson's desk.

"Are you certain it wouldn't be better for me to have it handy?" Watson asked.

"Quite," Mycroft responded.

Watson opened his desk drawer and placed the revolver inside then proceeded to shut and lock the desk.

"I won't be a trice," Watson said standing up from his desk. "I'll meet you at the curb."

Mycroft nodded and left Dr. Watson's home.

Chapter Twenty

Mycroft Holmes sat waiting in his carriage with the door open while his driver waited patiently on his perch atop the brougham for Dr. Watson to appear. It wasn't long before he left his home bag in hand, locked his front door behind him and walked quickly to the waiting four-wheeler.

"That was quite speedily done, Doctor," Mycroft observed as Watson entered the carriage carrying a simple travel case and his medical bag.

"Nothing out of the ordinary," Watson said taking his seat just as the carriage began to move. "I was used to quick packing from the Army and, of course, in my service to your brother."

"Old habits, eh, Doctor," Mycroft said.

"Indeed," Watson replied a little morosely.

The two men rode on in silence with Watson looking out the window at the passing street scenes of his beloved London. It seemed the antagonism between the two men had subsided greatly which added to the enjoyment of the ride. It wasn't too long a journey to the heart of London and the famed hotel.

"Northumberland Hotel," Mycroft's driver stated as the four-wheeler pulled to the curb in front of the building.

"The rooms are registered and paid for under the name 'Mr. Hamish,'" Mycroft stated as Dr. Watson grabbed his bags from where they rested on the carriage floor. "You may partake of any and all of the hotel's accommodations, Doctor."

"May I ask one more question, Mr. Holmes?" Watson asked before opening the carriage door.

Mycroft sighed, perturbed at the imposition, but nodded nonetheless.

"How is Inspector Lestrade involved in all of this?"

"He was with Sherlock on the case three years ago," Mycroft explained quickly. "We believe he was snatched to flush out the others currently still involved in the matter."

"That would include you?"

"Yes, as well as a few other operatives," Mycroft said. "And, unfortunately, now you."

"I see," Watson said and opened the carriage door.

"Three days, Doctor," Mycroft said. "A week on the outside and this should all be over. Enjoy yourself."

No sooner had Watson exited the four-wheeler than it was driven off while Mycroft was still shutting the door of the carriage.

Taking his bags, Watson marched quickly into the Northumberland and over to the front desk.

"How may I be of assistance, sir?" the clerk asked with a clipped almost military quality. He was a tall, gangly man of almost indeterminate age. He had a piercing gaze that would have been more in common with a police officer rather than someone who worked in a service capacity. His slicked back hair was done to perfection as though it was constantly maintained for accuracy.

"I believe there is a reservation for me?" Watson said. "Mr. Hamish?"

The clerk made a quick check of his records and immediately came upon the name.

"Ah, yes. Mr. Hamish, unlimited stay," the clerk said then glanced at Watson's meager baggage. "Visiting?"

"You might say that," Watson replied without wishing to provide too much information. "I plan on spending a lot of time in London for the foreseeable future."

"Mm-hmm," the clerk said with some suspicion and no attempt to hide it. "I'll just ring for someone to assist you with your...ahem...luggage."

Before Watson could object, the clerk swatted the bell on the desk and as if by magic a youth of about eleven years appeared wearing a red uniform.

"Please show Mr. Hamish to his suite," the clerk instructed handing the youth a key who nodded, pocketed the key then grabbed Watson's bags.

"Right this way, sir," the youth said and walked quickly toward the elevator.

Watson turned to the clerk. "Don't I need to sign in or anything?" Watson asked.

"All is taken care of, sir," the clerk said politely but still managed to sound bothered.

Watson followed the blond-haired boy in the red bell hop's uniform to the elevator just arriving on the ground floor almost as if on cue.

The boy entered the elevator carrying the bags and Watson joined him a moment later.

"The Grand Suite," the boy told the elderly elevator operator and a moment later the elevator doors were closing and the elevator was moving upward.

"What floor am I on?" Watson asked the youth.

"Top floor," the youth and the elevator operator stated at the same time.

"You have the whole floor, sir," the youth stated. "I've never seen this suite. It's rarely booked and when it is, the manager usually takes the guest to the room."

"Strange he'd have you do it, then," Watson said.

"It is a bit odd," the bell hop agreed.

"Well, you're in for a treat," Watson said. "You'll be able to brag to your cohorts."

The youth smiled broadly.

The elevator came to a slow stop and the attendant released the door.

The elevator opened onto a spacious foyer.

To the right of the elevator was a door accessing a stairwell leading back down to the other floors.

"That door stays locked from the outside," the boy said noticing Dr. Watson's observation of the stairs. "If you ring for room service or assistance, there is a buzzer next to your room door that will unlock the stairwell for access to this floor or it can be opened from your side if you wish to take the stairs."

"What about the elevator?" Watson asked just as the elevator doors closed encasing the attendant who disappeared within.

"The elevator can only be summoned by someone on this floor," the boy said and unlocked the door to the suite without ever lowering a bag to the floor.

The boy pushed open the door and stood aside for Dr. Watson to enter.

Dr. Watson walked into the suite and was stunned by the astounding luxury. Surely, this was what the palace must look like, he thought. Everything within appeared to have been freshly purchased and was spotless as if a thorough cleaning had been performed mere seconds before his arrival. There wasn't so much as a spot of dust or a wrinkle anywhere to be seen. There were two couches and a settee. There were two desks; one large with its own lamp and other amenities, writing paper, envelopes, ink well and pens, a large unused blotter, the other desk was much smaller and placed near the large windows to take in the light of the day.

"How often is this room rented?" Watson asked.

"Not often, sir," the boy stated and placed Dr. Watson's belongings near a door opposite the entrance.

"What's your name, lad?" Watson asked.

"Alfie, sir," the boy responded happy that a guest saw him as more than just another fixture in the hotel.

"Alfie, you seem to be a hard-working young fellow. Am I correct?"

"I like to think so, sir."

"Can you do some things for me?"

"Anything, sir," Alfie volunteered.

"Bring me...oh, say...two dozen telegram message forms and a London directory," Watson requested.

"Right away, sir," Alfie said and began quickly moving toward the entrance to the suite.

"One more thing, before you go," Watson said.

Alfie stopped in his tracks. "What's that, sir?" he asked.

"Where's the house telephone?"

Alfie indicated a telephone situated on a table near one of two overstuffed couches.

"Thank you, Alfie," Watson said.

Alfie dashed off closing the door behind him as he left.

Watson went to the house telephone and raised the receiver. It immediately began ringing on the other end.

"Front desk," came the reply from the clerk who had checked Watson in. "Of what service may I be to you, Mr.

Hamish?"

For a moment, Watson was surprised by the recognition of his "identity" but then realized it was possible this was the only room in the hotel to have a direct line to the desk or that the desk had a system for recognizing which room was ringing them.

"I'd like to have the assistance of the page boy, Alfie for a brief period of time," Watson stated. "Would there be a problem or an inconvenience to other guests if that were agreed upon?"

Watson couldn't care less if it made the rude clerk's job more inconvenient; in fact, he hoped it would, but he didn't want to trouble other guests.

"I think we can make an arrangement," the clerk said still politely but with an overpowering amount of rudeness. It truly was an art form in the way he said nothing troubling but managed to sound inconvenienced.

"Wonderful," Watson said sounding overly pleased. "He is on his way down to handle a request of mine. Please inform him his duties will be with me for the next few hours."

Without waiting for a reply, Watson hung up the house telephone and sat down in the chair behind the desk.

A few minutes later, Alfie buzzed the suite. Dr. Watson pressed the buzzer that allowed the stairwell door to be opened. A moment after that, Alfie knocked on the door.

"Come in," Watson said.

Alfie entered quite winded.

"Got what you asked for, sir," he said between gasps for air. "I was told to be at your beck and call for the next few hours."

"That's right," Watson said. "Did you run up the stairs to come here?"

"I did, sir," Alfie answered.

"Don't do that again," Watson said. "Use the elevator."

"Elevator is for guests, sir," Alfie stated. "We can only use it when we're assisting the guests, luggage and the like."

"Well, if I call for you, it's because I need you immediately," Watson said. "I expect you'll use the quickest way in the future. If there's a problem with your supervisor allowing it, you let me know and I will set him straight about my necessities."

Alfie smiled broadly. "I will, sir," he said. "Thank you."

Alfie handed Watson the telegram forms and the directory.

"Thank you, Alfie," Watson said taking the items and depositing them on the small desk near the large windows facing the street. "Come back in about half an hour and dressed in street clothes. I'll have some telegrams for you to send for me."

"Street clothes, sir?" Alfie asked confused.

"Yes," Watson said. "It won't do for someone to know where you've come from. This is kind of a secret errand."

"Half an hour," Alfie said smiling at the chance to be involved in a clandestine mission. "I will, sir. Street clothes."

"And bring something from the kitchen," Watson instructed. "Enough for two. Whatever you recommend."

Alfie smiled knowingly and Watson winked and smiled at the youth.

Alfie left allowing Dr. Watson to get to the task he'd assigned himself.

On the ride to the hotel with Mycroft Holmes, Watson had a little time to think over the events of the past few days, and the information Mycroft had provided. Mycroft was not aware Watson had found the telegram hidden in Lestrade's flat although

184

he was fairly certain he'd deduced as much since he'd met him at the Bagatelle Club. Thus, he was aware Watson knew of Ronald Adair. The telegram appeared to be a key piece of information and Watson reasoned this Adair fellow must bear a connection to the case in a special way. It was distinctly possible Adair was one of the operatives Mycroft had mentioned regarding the plot to overthrow the United States government and return it to British rule; actually rule by Professor James Moriarty.

Watson believed a talk with Ronald Adair would supply information that could conclude the whole matter and might even shed light on the location of Inspector Lestrade. But he would have to find a way of contacting Adair.

Watson opened the city directory to the first few pages under "A" to find the name "Adair."

"Nothing," he said aloud to himself. His voice was surprisingly loud in the quiet suite.

Next Watson checked the medical section of the London directory. He made a list of all of the physicians with offices in the area of the Bagatelle Club. He realized this would be a long shot but hoped Ronald Adair would have his doctor or at least a family practitioner somewhere near the club.

Seven doctors had offices near the club.

Watson wrote the same message on seven different blank message sheets.

"Medical emergency. Searching for Ronald Adair. Family member gravely ill. Respond only if you can assist."

Watson had to risk signing his true name to the telegrams. He would receive no response otherwise.

Alfie's knock at the door was a welcome sound after nearly thirty minutes of waiting for the lad.

Upon opening the door, Watson discovered Alfie in his simple street attire pushing a cart with a banquet atop it. There was baked chicken, steak and kidney pie, two types of potatoes, some type of rice dish and steamed broccoli as well as fresh baked bread and sweet butter. It smelled delicious and Watson's mouth began to water. He suddenly recalled he hadn't had a meal the likes of this one since his last dinner with Lestrade.

"Come in, young man," Watson said stepping out of Alfie's way. "You've really outdone yourself."

"Thank you, sir," Alfie said and guided the cart over to the large dining table on the opposite side of the spacious sitting room. He pulled plates and cups and utensils from beneath the top level of the cart and set the table for two.

"I asked the chef to make two of his favorite dishes," Alfie said as he began placing the food on the table. "This is what he provided, sir."

"It looks wonderful," Watson said taking a seat at the table. "You'll join me?"

"Join you, sir?" Alfie asked surprised. "I thought you might be expecting a guest."

"I was. You," Watson said and offered the second place setting to the lad.

"Thank you, sir," Alfie nearly shouted. "It would be my honor."

Watson and Alfie shared a delightful meal together wherein Watson learned Alfie was the sole breadwinner for his family; a mother and two sisters. His father had been killed some years earlier in a mining accident in Kent, and his mother had recently fallen ill and lost her job as a maid at the hotel. She'd been able to get Alfie his position prior to her leaving. Alfie had hopes of being a police officer when he was older but didn't know how to begin training for such a position.

"I think I might be able to help you with some of that," Watson told the youth to his great pleasure. "I have a number of connections over at Scotland Yard."

"Really, sir?" Alfie said excited. "I wouldn't know how to thank you. You don't even know me. Why would you want to help someone like me?"

"What do you mean by that?" Watson asked.

"Someone who is below you, sir," he said a little saddened. "Status-wise."

"Alfie," Watson said compassionately. "I see a young man who works hard and does a good job. Why would I not want to help someone like that?"

"Well," Alfie said. "I've met a lot of people who stay at this hotel; some in this very suite, and none of them even gave me a second look. I was just the boy who carried their luggage and opened their doors and hailed their cabs. That's all. People who can afford to stay in rooms like these don't really see people like me."

"That is their loss, then," Watson said. "They miss out on the truly colorful people of this city when they ignore others."

"Well, it's a kindness you do for me, sir," Alfie said. "I am happy to perform some for you."

"Well, I want you to wrap up the rest of this food and take it home to your family," Watson said to Alfie's delight. "You can start by doing that."

"Happy to, sir," he said.

"I also want you to accept my apologies for not being completely honest with you," Watson continued and saw the look

187

of disappointment instantly cross Alfie's face.

"I am not truly a guest in your hotel, young man," Watson continued. "I have to stay here because of an investigation I'm involved in."

"Are you a policeman?" Alfie asked excited.

"No, not a policeman," Watson explained. "My real name is Dr. John Watson. I used to work with Mr. Sherlock Holmes."

Alfie was stunned.

"Are you all right, Alfie?" Watson asked noticing the color run out of the boy's face.

"I...I..." Alfie stuttered and reached into the pocket of his worn jacket where he withdrew a battered book that had obviously been read over and over.

"You're this man?" Alfie said placing the book on the table. "This Dr. John Watson?"

Watson looked at the old book. It was a copy of Beeton's Christmas Annual which carried the first adventure he had shared with Sherlock Holmes titled "A Study in Scarlet."

"Yes," Watson said with a smile. "I am THAT Dr. Watson.

Alfie leaned back in his chair. Watson was certain he would have passed out had he been standing.

"I never thought..." Alfie began. "I never imagined I would ever meet you or Mr. Holmes. I wanted to. I found out you were here once to visit a guest, Baskerman, or something, **(22)** but I was just a wee lad then and I wasn't working here. My mother was still providing for us kids then. When I got this job a friend told me you'd been here, once upon a time, and now...now..."

Alfie lost his ability to speak again.

"Alfie," Watson said reassuringly. "I'm just a regular man like any other. I put my trousers on one leg at a time just like you or just like any prince. There is nothing supernatural about me or about anyone else who might be considered famous which I most certainly do not consider myself."

Alfie suddenly sprung to life. "No!" he contradicted. "No. That's not true. You are famous. A writer. You worked with Sherlock Holmes; the great detective."

"I know," Watson said trying to calm the boy. "And he was just a man too. He was just very, very smart."

This seemed to dishearten the boy.

"Why do you carry that book with you?" Watson continued trying to steer the conversation away from hero worship.

"I study it," Alfie said. "I use it like a text book. Because I want to be a policeman and not just "the best of a bad lot" like Mr. Holmes said. I've been rereading his...your...story "A Study in Scarlet" to learn about deductive reasoning and be more observant. I'm not very good."

"I will hazard a guess you're better than you think," Watson said.

"If I was any good, I would have been able to figure out who you were before you told me," Alfie said disappointed.

"And how would you have done that?" Watson asked.

"Well," Alfie said. "I would have noticed your medical bag. That would have told me you were a doctor. The callous on your right hand would have told me about your writing. The way you stand and walk shows you were in the military. You mentioned in the story that you'd been a military doctor. Probably a few more things, but those are what I noticed."

189

Watson began to laugh and continued to do so, until his head began to ache.

Alfie looked a little chastised.

"I'm not laughing at you, Alfie," Watson said when he'd finally regained his composure. "You don't know how amusing that was for me. I thank you greatly, my young friend."

"Was I wrong about my observations?" Alfie asked embarrassed at the possibility he had appeared idiotic.

"Not at all, my boy," Watson said reassuringly. "Not at all. In fact, you were right on all accounts. Very well done. Very well done, indeed."

"Then why were you laughing?"

"Again, not at you, lad. It's just I haven't heard words spoken to me in that way in three years. They were refreshing and cleansing to my spirit. You have done me a great service without the intention of knowing you were performing it. Thank you, again."

"I'm glad I could make you feel better," Alfie said still a bit confused.

"Alfie," Watson said. "I am here because the British Government has placed me here."

"Are you a spy?" Alfie asked conspiratorially. "Are you on a mission?"

"No," Watson said. "More of a well-attended prisoner."

Alfie's eyes widened again in surprise.

"I'm not a danger," Watson said reassuringly. "At least not to you. The powers-that-be want me out of the way while they finish up an investigation."

"Were you interfering with them?"

"Well, they say I was, but now, I'm not so sure."

"How can I help?"

"You've helped greatly already," Watson said with a smile. "But I am still in need of further assistance. I'm going to need you to send the telegrams I have on the desk, and I want them sent from outside the hotel."

"We have a telegraph office downstairs, sir," Alfie said moving back into his page persona.

"I know, but these cables will have my actual name on them and the responses will come to Dr. John Watson. I can't have anyone knowing I'm staying here. That's the reason I asked you to change into street clothes instead of your uniform. Understand?"

Alfie nodded.

"Now, pack up this food and grab those cables," Watson said standing. "Is there a telegraph office between here and your home?"

"Two," Alfie said as he packed food into cardboard cartons he retrieved from beneath the trolley he'd wheeled the meal in with. "One a little out of the way."

"You can use the nearest one," Watson said and removed a change purse from his pocket. Opening it he removed two gold sovereigns and handed them to Alfie.

"Take these to cover the cost of the cables," Watson said. "If the office is busy, use a little extra to grease the wheels and get those sent quickly."

"Shall I wait for a response, Doctor?" Alfie asked.

"No," Watson said. "But stop at the telegraph office before coming to work tomorrow morning and bring me any responses they might have received."

"Will do," Alfie said.

With the food placed carefully into two containers and a pocket full of telegram messages, Alfie left Dr. Watson's company.

Watson locked the door behind Alfie and sighed.

Was this the right path to follow? He wondered. Was he truly doing the right thing in pursuing this matter now that Mycroft Holmes had brought him up to speed?

It was a tough dilemma. Watson had no doubt it would keep him up during the night.

He was wrong.

The good food provided by the hotel's chef and the good company provided by the young page, Alfie, plus the exhaustion he felt and the wonderfully comfortable accommodations of the Northumberland Hotel were enough to knock him out at almost the exact moment he climbed into bed and his head hit the pillow.

Chapter Twenty-One

Watson awoke to the insistent pounding on the door somewhere in his immediate vicinity. For a brief moment he couldn't recall where he was. His surroundings were completely foreign to him. Then the events of the previous day flooded into his mind. He was at the Northumberland Hotel at the expense of British Government; being kept out of sight and out of mind.

He quickly got out of bed, grabbed the complimentary dressing gown from the hook on the bedroom door and put it on over his night clothes. Then he dashed to the hotel room door.

"Alfie," Watson said surprised to see the youth. "So early?"

"Early?" Alfie said confused. "It's nearly eight in the morning. I got here at six. I've made two visits up here, but you never answered my knock and the front desk claimed you hadn't left the hotel. I was getting worried. I thought something may have happened to you."

"I'm sorry, my young friend," Watson said and motioned for the boy to enter. "You have some word for me, I take it?"

"First things first, Doctor. Are you all right?" Alfie asked obviously concerned and entering the suite.

"I'm fine," Watson said shutting the door. "I must have been a bit more exhausted than I thought. Slept like a baby last night. First time in...well, in a long time."

"I was about to get the pass key and open the door myself," Alfie said finally allowing himself to relax and calm down. He'd obviously had an intense scare when no one answered the door.

"Well," Watson said reassuringly. "As you can see, I'm

fine. Now..."

"Oh!" Alfie blurted reaching into his vest. "Your telegram."

"Tele...GRAM?" Watson asked slightly surprised.

"Yes, sir," Alfie said retrieving the response and handing it to Dr. Watson. "Just one response...so far. I'll check with the telegram office later today to see if there've been any others."

Watson opened the envelope.

"You didn't open it?" he asked.

"No, sir," Alfie said. "Why would I?"

"I assumed you would."

"Never," Alfie claimed. "It doesn't involve me. I'm just the page boy."

"And my partner," Watson said with a wry smile.

"Your..." Alfie said surprised.

"It's from a Dr. Jonas Wilheimer who claims he has a female patient named Adair. I was looking for a male."

"Does that help?" Alfie asked.

"It might," Watson said thinking. "It might."

Watson took the telegram over to the table and sat down.

"Have you breakfasted, Alfie?" he asked the youth.

"No, sir," he answered. "I wanted to get a jump on things this morning. I didn't know I'd have so much extra time."

"Again, my apologies," Watson said. "Would you be able to get me some toast, jam and tea and something for yourself?"

"With pleasure," Alfie said. "And speaking of food, my family thanks you for the fine meal you provided them last evening."

"Tell them they're more than welcome when you see them," Watson replied. "Meanwhile, get that breakfast order to the chef and be back up here as soon as you can."

"Right, Doctor," he said and in a moment he was gone.

Watson retrieved the directory he'd used the night before and located Dr. Wilheimer's address.

He made a note of it on the telegram's envelope then placed it on the table and went to dress for the day. He planned a visit to Dr. Wilheimer's office before the noon hour as soon as he and Alfie were done with breakfast.

Chapter Twenty-Two

Breakfast for Watson consisted of the toast and jam he had ordered and some God awful concoction that was presumably tea. No amount of milk and sugar was able to revive it. Alfie on the other hand enjoyed three fried eggs and what appeared to be all of the bacon taken from an entire pig.

Watson ate slowly and advised young Alfie of his plans of the morning.

"So, you won't be needing me then, Doctor," Alfie said.

"I'd like you to hail a cab for me," Watson said, "but I think that will be the extent of your duties until I return."

"You're sure you don't want me to accompany you?"

Watson smiled.

"I'll be fine on this errand," he told Alfie. "But the cab I will need should not be the first one you come across, not even the second in line. Go to the third and request that one." **(23)**

"Why, Doctor?" Alfie asked.

"It's a...precaution," Watson said and would say no more.

Alfie nodded as if he understood and left the suite. Watson gathered up the information on the telegram and grabbed his medical bag as added authenticity when he called upon Dr. Wilheimer.

*　　*　　*

Dr. Watson discovered Alfie had flagged down a hansom cab from down the street which was now waiting for him in front of the hotel. The driver appeared to show impatience in having to wait but immediately brightened when he realized his fare had finally arrived.

"You did as I instructed?" Watson said in a hushed tone

in Alfie's ear.

"Absolutely, sir," Alfie responded in the same whisper.
"Third in line."

"Wonderful," Watson said and climbed into the open cab.
"I will see you this evening, my young friend. You may go about
your regular duties until I return."

Alfie nodded.

"Where to, sir?" the cabby asked.

"Drive for a bit, if you will, cabby," Watson instructed
and the cab left the curb.

A moment later a four-wheeler from across the street and
facing in the opposite direction, turned around and begin to
follow the hansom carrying Dr. Watson. The driver's face was
hidden from view by the heavy scarf covering it.

Alfie failed to observe.

* * *

"Any idea of a destination yet, guv?" the cabby asked
after a couple of minutes of riding aimlessly through the city. "If
it's a tour you're looking for, I can provide some of London's
highlights for you. Buckingham Palace, Trafalgar Square, and
the like."

"No, thank you, cabby," Watson said withdrawing the
telegram from his pocket and checking the address for Dr.
Wilheimer. "You can take me to Forty-two Devonshire Mews
West, near Harley Street."

"Right, sir," the cabby said and made a left turn on the
first available street.

It took slightly more than twenty minutes to reach the
address on Devonshire Mews.

"Will you be kind enough to wait for me?" Watson asked

as he disembarked from the hansom. "I'm sure I won't be long."

"Happy to, guv," the cabby responded.

Watson climbed the four steps that led off the sidewalk to Dr. Wilheimer's door and rang the bell.

A young and quite attractive housekeeper answered the door. Her hair was a striking auburn color and her green eyes shown brightly in the morning light.

"Is Dr. Wilheimer available?" Dr. Watson asked.

"I believe he is just finishing with a patient," the lovely young woman said. "This way."

She moved aside so Watson could enter and she led him to a small sitting room where she offered an uncomfortable chair for him to sit on while he waited.

"May I tell him who's calling?" she asked.

Watson provided her with one of his calling cards. Then she left without another word leaving behind a faint odor of lilac and a pleasant memory of her beauty.

In a few minutes, Dr. Wilheimer entered rolling his shirt sleeves back down over his arms. When he finished he straightened his waistcoat and brushed some dust away from his trousers. Watson began to rise but Wilheimer motioned for him to remain sitting and Watson did so lamenting having to remain in the uncomfortable chair.

"Good morning, Dr. Watson," Dr. Wilheimer said quite pleasantly. "I am in receipt of your telegram, of course. How can I be of assistance?"

"As I stated, this is a medical emergency," Watson nervously embellished. "I'm trying to find a Ronald Adair. There's been a tragedy in the northern country, and I've been charged with contacting the next of kin."

"I wasn't aware the Adairs had relations in the north country," Wilheimer stated.

"I'm not sure they are related either," Watson said growing increasingly uncomfortable with the ruse. "Which is why I'd like to reach out to them...just in case."

"How did you come by their name?"

"A doctor friend of mine," Watson said. "From that area. Knew I was in harness here in London. He thought I could help."

"Who might this 'doctor friend' be?" Wilheimer asked beginning to show some suspicion.

"Doyle," Watson said blurting out the first name to come to mind. "Originally from Edinburgh." **(24)**

Wilheimer stared at Dr. Watson and Watson began to worry this was not going to go well.

"Can't say I've heard of him," Wilheimer stated.

Watson shrugged not knowing what to say.

"As you know," Wilheimer continued. "It's not our practice to give out information on patients, except in consultations."

Watson nodded.

"You'd be assisting me a great deal," Watson said and paused to stare directly into the other doctor's eyes and presenting a sincere request. "You have no idea how great."

Wilheimer took a moment then went to his desk. He searched through an index he kept in a desk drawer and opened it to the very beginning presumably where the A's were listed. With a handy pencil he jotted down a note on a piece of paper, replaced the index in the desk drawer and handed the note over to Dr. Watson.

"You understand I can't provide you with medical

information on anyone I'm currently treating," Wilheimer stated handing the note to Watson. "All that is, is an address."

"That's all I've asked for," Watson said placing the note in his inside coat pocket.

"Then I hope it helps," Wilheimer said still not losing his tone of suspicion. "You can show yourself out?"

Watson nodded and made a hasty retreat from the room.

Outside Dr. Wilheimer's practice, Watson took the opportunity to draw a deep breath of relief. He'd lost his wife, Inspector Lestrade had disappeared, Mycroft Holmes had chastised him...twice, his greatest friend had deceived him about certain incidents, he'd been shot at, and still he hadn't felt nearly the discomfort as he did during those few short minutes with Dr. Wilheimer.

Finally, Watson climbed into the cab still waiting for him. Once seated in the hansom, he withdrew the note from his pocket.

"Ninety-four Park Lane, driver," Watson said and the cabby whipped up the horse and they were off. It wasn't until they'd traveled a distance down the street that Watson finally began to relax from the tension of the last few minutes.

With his mind clearing of apprehension he began to think about what he was going to say to Ronald Adair. He'd prepared nothing for this interview. He couldn't use the emergency in the north country or the fictional illness of another family member. Adair would see through the ruse immediately. It would have to be the truth and nothing more. Perhaps he could use the name of Mycroft Holmes to gain entry. If young Adair was indeed working for the British Empire in conjunction with the American government, the use of Mycroft's name could gain him access.

In the end, it would not be necessary

Chapter Twenty-Three

Watson's hansom pulled to a stop in front of Ninety-four Park Lane.

Watson exited the cab and stood looking at the address next to the door and down at the note he held ascertaining he'd arrived at the correct address.

"Still want me to wait, guv?" the cabby asked.

"If I am not out in ten minutes," Watson said and handed the cabby his fair and a hefty tip. "You may leave. But please give me a few minutes time before you do."

"Right you are, guv," the cabby said with a smile as he looked approvingly at the money Watson had provided him.

Watson walked to the front door of the Adair house and rang the doorbell.

The door was answered by yet another well-dressed butler with slicked back black hair and a pencil thin mustache who stood rigidly at attention with an almost deferential demeanor causing Watson to wonder if all of London's servants were trained at the same facility in order to present such a similar introduction.

"Dr. Watson to see Ronald Adair," Watson said and presented this butler with another medical card. "I have no appointment, but I think he will wish to hear what I have to say."

The butler glanced at the card and silently stood aside for Dr. Watson to enter the home.

Inside, the butler closed the door behind Watson and walked off into the interior of the home. It was only a few moments later that an easy-going young man, dressed casually and smiling broadly, appeared from somewhere within the house.

"Could I be being visited by THE Dr. Watson of the Sherlock Holmes stories?" the young man asked hopefulness gleaming in his sparkling blue eyes.

"I bare that distinction," Watson responded pleasantly. "Have I the pleasure of addressing Mr. Ronald Adair?"

"You do, Doctor," he stated with a slight bow. "But it is I who have the pleasure. Please, follow me into the sitting room. I've already requested tea."

Happily, Watson followed the young Adair into a sitting room and took the offered chair; a much more comfortable version of the one he'd sat in at Dr. Wilheimer's residence. In fact, the whole room seemed more comfortable and welcoming leading Watson to believe it was a woman who'd been responsible for the pleasing décor and harmonious arrangement of the furniture.

"It's an honor to have you in my home," Adair continued praising his guest. "I've been a great admirer of your work and that of your friend for some time. I especially enjoyed *The Sign of the Four*. What an amazing adventure."

"Thank you," Watson said growing a bit somber at recalling that mystery involved the two people he held dearest in his life. "But I must tell you that Sherlock Holmes--"

"Is...gone," Adair interrupted. "I know. I read of his passing some years ago. A tragedy, really. My condolences."

"Thank you," Watson said.

"I do hope you have some more adventures yet to be set to paper for some future publication?" Adair said more hopefully.

"Indeed," Watson said. "There are a few adventures that I may still set down in the future."

"Wonderful!" Adair cheered. "I'll be the first to obtain a

published copy."

"Thank you," Watson said hoping to soon direct the conversation to his true reason for visiting.

Just then, the maid, a dainty young thing with straight blond hair tied in a bun, entered carrying a tray with a steaming tea pot, cups, milk, sugar and some sort of biscuit. Watson passed on the biscuit but accepted the tea and some sugar.

"So," Adair said sipping from his own tea following the departure of the maid. "What brings you to my door?"

"I've recently been looking into a matter that involves Scotland Yard, that I think you might be able to assist me with," Watson said confidently.

"Me?" Adair asked surprised. "How so?"

"You're aware of the disappearance of Inspector Lestrade some three days ago?"

"Inspector who?"

"Lestrade," Watson said with burgeoning confusion. "The man you've been working with recently."

"I haven't been working with anyone from Scotland Yard, Dr. Watson," Adair said and set his tea cup down on the table before him. "I have nothing to do with the police in any capacity. Are you certain you have the correct person?"

"You've not been involved in an espionage case involving the possible overthrow of the United States Government?"

Adair sat stunned for a moment then laughed loudly.

"Have I said something humorous?" Watson asked.

"Haven't you?" Adair said still laughing. "This is a joke right? Did Perkins at the club put you up to this? Some sort of April Fools' Day prank? A few days early, but..."

"Mr. Adair, I assure you--"

"It's a good one," Adair said interrupting Dr. Watson's protestations. "Missing police inspector. Espionage plot. Really quite good."

Watson reached into his jacket pocket and removed the telegram found at Lestrade's flat. He handed it to Adair, but it did nothing other than reinforce the laughter.

"Oh my," Adair said as he regained control of his mirth. "This is really well done. Tell Perkins I said so. Props and everything. I don't know who you really are, but you're a terrific actor. Stalwart. Serious. You don't break character, do you?"

"I--" Watson started.

"Well done, indeed," Adair said and stood.

"Unfortunately, I haven't much time to afford you in continuing the prank. You can see yourself out, I presume?"

Adair walked out of the room leaving Dr. Watson shocked at the odd turn of events.

This was supposed to open the floodgates of information for him, but instead he'd been left feeling foolish and stupid.

Watson set down his tea cup and left the house.

Outside, his cab was gone.

Watson hailed the first one that presented itself.

"The Northumberland Hotel," Watson instructed his driver without giving the man a second glance or noticing he had a scarf wrapped closely around his face. Instead, Watson climbed into the cab and was almost instantly whisked away in the direction of the hotel.

Chapter Twenty-Four

"You have a message, Mr. Hamish," the annoying desk clerk said to Dr. Watson upon his entry to the lobby. He lifted a plain envelope and waved it slightly in the air as one might do a treat to a well-trained dog. Watson walked over to the front desk and took the envelope from the clerk.

It was sealed shut but otherwise blank. No address. No name. Not even the name of the hotel.

"How do you know this is for me?" Watson asked looking at both sides of the envelope as if he could have missed something.

"That is what the messenger told me," the clerk said in his professional, clipped manner as if it were the most apparent fact in the known universe and while continuing to handle some paperwork for the hotel.

"Messenger?" Watson asked looking for a bit of clarification.

"Yes, Mr. Hamish," the clerk said exasperated and ceasing his report filing. "A young boy came in, removed that envelope from his satchel, handed it to me and stated 'For Mr. Hamish.'"

"Did he say anything else?"

"Like what?"

"Like who it was from or from where it was sent?"

"I assume that information will be within," the clerk said sarcastically and nodded at the envelope. He then scooped up his paperwork and began placing different sheets into different cubbyholes behind the desk.

Watson walked off toward the lift.

Recognizing Watson as a prominent guest of the hotel, the elevator operator immediately set the lift in operation and took him to the top floor suite. There was no conversation between the two men as Watson was intent on examining the envelope and waited patiently to reach his room before opening it.

No address, either of the hotel or the location whence it came.

No markings, watermarks, maker's insignia, nothing.

It was simply a plane white envelope.

"Have a good evening, sir," the lift operator stated upon reaching Watson's floor.

"Thank you," Watson said. "You as well."

Watson left the lift and crossed to his door. He heard the doors to the lift close behind him as he retrieved his room key from his vest pocket.

Once inside the suite, Watson walked to the desk. He removed the telegram from his jacket pocket and placed it on the desk. Then he used the Northumberland Hotel provided letter opener to slit the envelope carefully open. Inside was a newspaper clipping.

Watson removed the clipping and recognized it immediately as one he'd seen many times from three years earlier. It was from the London Times and it read "Sherlock Holmes Dead!" in large type.

Across the headline written with a red pencil were the words "The Game is Afoot?" Like some kind of cryptic question. Or some sort of mocking? But who would do this? Who would be so cruel as to dredge up one of the worst times of Watson's life? Why would someone hold on to an old newspaper headline? What was this missive meant to do?

Watson became furious.

"If this were some kind of action by that horse's ass at the front desk," Watson said to himself. "I'll see to it he's turned out on the street and make certain he never works in this city again."

But what would be the clerk's motive in playing such a prank?

Watson was certain the clerk didn't intentionally want to make an enemy of him. His rudeness was probably just his way. More than likely, this was his natural demeanor, like it or not. He was probably extremely efficient at his duties and a little gruffness was nothing to be upset about.

Slowly Watson began to calm himself.

Unfortunately, he was still stuck with the suspicious message.

What could it mean? What was the purpose? What was it trying to tell him?

"The Game is Afoot?" Watson read aloud. "Why is this a question? Whenever Holmes used the phrase it was as a statement."

Holmes, Watson thought. If only Holmes were with me now. He'd make sense out of all of this.

A thought suddenly screamed its way into Watson's head. One so shocking it actually startled him for a moment.

"Holmes," Watson said aloud. "It's ridiculous...absurd."

A knock at the door of the suite brought Watson out of his reverie.

"Who is it?" he asked through the closed door.

"Alfie, sir," the voice of the page boy announced. "Brought up some dinner."

Watson opened the door and ushered the boy into the

room. Immediately, he noticed the table was cluttered with a number of dishes containing more food than the two of them could possibly eat in an evening or possibly even a fortnight of evenings.

"What's all this?" Watson asked looking surprisingly at the feast.

"I didn't know what you'd be in the mood for," Alfie said as he wheeled the food cart over to the dining table then began setting it for two places. "I also took the opportunity to have something fixed for myself. I hope you don't mind, sir."

"Not at all, Alfie," Watson said and sat down at the table. "I'm actually very hungry. Thank you for thinking ahead."

Alfie served the meal which included a creamy soup with mushrooms, steamed asparagus, a cheese souffle which wasn't to Dr. Watson's liking but was immensely enjoyed by Alfie who had three helpings, and a pork roast.

Both ate a bit more than their fill at the dinner table and for a short while, Watson was able to forget about the woes he was facing and enjoy the company of this kind youth.

As with the previous meal, Watson insisted Alfie take home the remaining food to his family and judged the portions were extra-large possibly just for that purpose.

"I wonder if I might bounce something off you, Alfie," Watson said when the boy was finished packing the food in the cardboard containers he'd brought to take the remnants home.

"Certainly, sir," Alfie said eagerly. "Happy to help."

"You know what became of my friend, Sherlock Holmes. Am I correct?" Watson said.

"He died fighting with the Professor. Went over a cliff, didn't he?"

"Yes," Watson said without being able to completely disguise his melancholy over the horrible memory. "However, his body was never found, nor that of Professor Moriarty for that matter, but in this case the final resting place of the Professor is immaterial. Understand?

"It doesn't matter," Alfie said.

"Correct."

"Are you saying they might not be dead?" Alfie said. "No bodies. No deaths?"

"For the sake of this discussion, let's limit ourselves only to Sherlock Holmes."

"All right," Alfie agreed. "Do you think Mr. Holmes is still alive?"

"Let me present you with some evidence and you tell me what you would think, before I tell you my interpretation."

Alfie nodded.

Watson told Alfie of the final days he'd spent with his friend, the great detective, Sherlock Holmes. He described the way Holmes had shown up at his home while his wife was out, and about the case he'd been working on to destroy the greatest criminal empire the world had ever known, even though most of the actions taken were unknown to the general public.

"So the Professor's men set fire to Mr. Holmes's house?" Alfie asked sitting in rapt suspense as Dr. Watson related the Adventure of the Final Problem.

"That's what I was told," Watson said.

Watson went on to say the rooms in Baker Street were fine, and the rent had been paid by Mr. Holmes's brother Mycroft for the past three years.

"Why would Sherlock Holmes lie to you?" Alfie asked.

"Why indeed," Watson replied. "Then there are these."

Watson retrieved the telegram found in Inspector Lestrade's flat and the newspaper clipping that arrived at the front desk and handed them to Alfie.

Alfie studied both pieces of paper.

"Do you think, the 'H' on the telegram is supposed to be from Mr. Sherlock Holmes and not his brother?" he asked.

"Originally, I did, for but a moment, then dismissed it because I knew Sherlock Holmes was dead. I'd decided it had come from his brother, Mycroft."

"But what do you think now?"

"Now?" Watson asked and ran a hand through his hair as he paced the room. "I don't know."

Alfie looked at the newspaper clipping.

"Holmes used to say," Watson continued. "'When you have eliminated the impossible, whatever remains, however improbable, must be the truth.' **(23)** There was never a recovery of Sherlock Holmes's body from the bottom of the Reichenbach Falls. Granted, that is a nearly impossible task, but a search was done as best as could be and...nothing was ever found. Is it possible he never went over the falls? Is it possible Mycroft Holmes has known of his brother's survival these last three years and has kept the rooms in Baker Street in order so that someday he might return to them? Is it possible that Inspector Lestrade had been working with Sherlock Holmes for some time prior to his disappearance and that's why he suddenly became so successful at his career? Are any of these things possible, Alfie?"

Alfie shook his head as if all of this information was almost too much for him to take in.

"What do you think, Doctor?" he asked. "Would

Sherlock Holmes not tell you he was alive? You were his best friend. Would he fake his death and not tell his best friend?"

"I would like to think not," Watson said contemplating. "But I think I might be too close to this matter. That's why I'm asking your opinion."

"Would there be a reason to keep you in the dark, if he had somehow survived?"

"My personal safety, perhaps, or that of my wife."

"Then to him, it would be logical not to inform you of the true events with his enemy at the cliff. Am I right?"

"Alfie," Watson said with an understanding smile. "I think you are right."

Watson sighed and realized he'd overdone his eating by a little more than a bit. He was now very tired and wished only for a bath and then bed.

"Thank you for your all of assistance tonight, my lad," Watson told Alfie with a weak smile. "You are dismissed. I hope your family enjoys the food."

"They will, sir," Alfie said returning the smile. "Thank you again."

"It's my pleasure."

Watson assisted Alfie with clearing the table and placing everything back on the cart, then gently escorted the youth from the suite.

Before retiring for the night, Watson decided to make a list of the facts of the case as he saw them. Taking pen and paper from the writing desk in the room, Watson listed:

    1. No body found at Reichenbach Falls
    2. No fire at 221B Baker Street as Holmes

reported
3. Rooms at 221B have been preserved
4. Mycroft Holmes pays the rent at 221B
5. Lestrade's recent crime solving success at Scotland Yard
6. Telegram signed "H"
7. Newspaper clipping with "The Game Is Afoot" handwritten upon it

"When you have eliminated the impossible," Watson said to himself. "Whatever remains, must be the truth." **(25)**

He placed the telegram and the newspaper clipping with the list and left them on the desk.

"Holmes is alive," Watson said aloud to himself and smiled. For the first time since before Mary's illness and subsequent demise, Dr. Watson smiled while he was alone. "Sherlock Holmes is alive."

Watson retired to the sleeping chamber and slept soundly through the night.

Chapter Twenty-Five

The following morning, Watson rose early and prepared for his day. He'd decided the night before just prior to falling asleep that he would get the answers he needed and didn't care whose toes he had to step on to do it. Nothing in Heaven or on Earth was going to prevent him from discovering the truth.

His first stop was going to be 221B Baker Street and another visit with his former long-suffering landlady, Mrs. Hudson. Although he did not relish the thought of stepping on her toes to get his answers, he was willing to put a little pressure on the woman as there was a slight chance she was somehow involved in the deception of what had really occurred in Baker Street on Holmes's last night in residence some three years earlier.

Watson met young Alfie in the lobby and couldn't help noticing the glare he'd received from the always ornery and ever-present desk clerk. What was with that man, Watson wondered.

"I'll need another cab this morning, Alfie," Watson told the bell boy.

"Same as before, sir?" Alfie asked conspiratorially. "Not the first or second, but the third in line?"

"I see no reason to drop our preventative measures now," Watson said. "Do you?"

"No, sir," Alfie replied eager to assist and was off and out the main entrance in a flash.

Watson waited until he saw the cab pull to a stop in front of the hotel, then he exited stealing a glance behind him to see the clerk still staring at him.

Outside Watson thanked Alfie and climbed into the cab.

"Two Twenty-One B Baker Street, cabbie," Watson said and the cab was away.

Watson pulled from his jacket pocket the sheet of paper where he'd jotted down his notes and the telegram and newspaper clipping and went over them once more. If not Sherlock Holmes, who could be responsible for these missives, he wondered. He was hoping Mrs. Hudson would be able to shed a little more light upon the matter, but he was nearly certain she couldn't be involved in a conspiracy to hide the truth about Sherlock Holmes's death from him. Chances were she was as much in the dark about her old tenant as Watson was. Still, had she never thought to even ask Mycroft Holmes why he would wish to preserve his brother's quarters and never visit them? That in itself seemed odd on her part. Watson was now aware she didn't need the money as she had other properties that allowed for income. Why had she agreed to keep the rooms in Baker Street vacant and preserved? Was she somehow agreeing to perpetuate the memory of the world's first and only consulting detective? Surely that would be nonsensical as well. If she and Mycroft were preserving the rooms for some future memorial, wouldn't they have taken steps to display it by now? It'd been three years. How much longer were they willing to wait?

And yet, if Sherlock Holmes were secretly still residing there after somehow surviving the battle with Moriarty at the Reichenbach Falls, it would answer all of Watson's questions and suspicions. So many "somehows?"

Eventually, the cab pulled to a stop in front of Watson's old rooms. Watson paid the driver and added a generous tip.

"Thank you, guvnor," the cabby said in a gravelly voice. "Would ye be wanting me to wait for ye?"

"No, thank you, cabby," Watson said and mounted the steps to his former boarding house.

"Have a good day, sir," the cabby called out and whipped up his horse pulling away from the curb.

Baker Street was very quiet. There was no pedestrian traffic and no other cabs save the one that had just left; the horse's hooves echoing ominously on the empty street. Even the early birds of spring seemed to have held their tongues for the moment. It was strange and almost foreboding.

Watson rang the bell, and a moment later was greeted by the smiling face of his former landlady.

"Dr. Watson," she nearly shrieked with glee throwing the front door wide open. "What a lovely surprise. Please, come in."

She stood aside to allow Dr. Watson to enter then closed the door behind him.

Inside, the Doctor removed his hat and handed it to the pleasant landlady. She placed it on a hook just inside the doorway and ushered her former tenant into the sitting room where he took a seat on the settee near a short table.

"Some tea, for you, Doctor?" she offered.

"Yes, Mrs. Hudson," he said. "That would be nice. There's still a bit of a winter chill in the air."

"I've noticed," she said. "Spring is surely taking its sweet time getting here this year."

Mrs. Hudson left the room and returned a few moments later with the tea and some bakery confections that appeared to contain fruit fillings.

"I had just taken the kettle off the burner when you rang the bell," she said setting the tray down on the short table near the settee and taking a seat in a chair opposite Dr. Watson.

"Do you still take it with two sugars, Doctor?"

"Precisely," Watson said and patiently watched as Mrs. Hudson prepared his tea.

"What brings you here today, might I ask?" she said handing Watson his cup and saucer. "A patient in the area?"

"No," Watson said a bit nervously. "Nothing like that."

"Please do try one of my pastries," Mrs. Hudson said offering the plate to Watson.

Watson took one and placed it in the saucer next to his steaming tea cup.

"This isn't easy for me to say, Mrs. Hudson," Watson stated, breaking eye contact with his former landlady and setting his cup and saucer down on the table. "I'm not one to confront people I know and love with a belief I've been lied to."

"Lied to?" Mrs. Hudson said shocked. "Who's lied to you?"

Watson drew in and released a mighty sigh.

"You have," he said.

"Dr. Watson," Mrs. Hudson said visibly wounded. "I can assure you--"

"Is Sherlock Holmes living here or not?" Watson demanded interrupting his former landlady.

"He is not," Mrs. Hudson said firmly but with sudden sadness in her voice. "And I do not appreciate being called a liar."

"Then why are his rooms being kept as they were when he lived here?"

"I told you. Mr. Mycroft Holmes has been paying the rent. Those are his wishes to keep the rooms preserved."

"And you haven't thought to ask him why he wants the

rooms maintained without his ever visiting?"

"If he ever visited, I would ask him," Mrs. Hudson said regaining some of her resolve. "But he doesn't visit. At least not until..."

Mrs. Hudson covered her mouth.

"Not until what, Mrs. Hudson?" Watson demanded.

"I've said too much," she responded.

"You've said nothing of which I'm not already aware," Watson said. He was growing angry and desperate. It was becoming a battle to control his temper in this matter, and Watson feared he would take it out on Mrs. Hudson. This woman was more than a simple landlady. She was a trusted friend for over a decade. How could he doubt she'd ever tell him anything but the truth? But the evidence was growing that Sherlock Holmes was alive and probably living at 221B Baker Street.

"I was told not to speak to anyone about it, especially you," Mrs. Hudson explained.

Watson immediately quieted his rage. He wasn't going to get anywhere trying to intimidate Mrs. Hudson. He would have to approach her as a longtime friend.

"I'm sorry, Mrs. Hudson," Watson said with actual emotion and empathy. "I was wrong. I should have never doubted your integrity. I shouldn't have gotten angry with you."

After a moment, Mrs. Hudson replied, "It's all right, Doctor. You've been through so much over the last month. It's bound to take a toll on a body."

Watson nodded.

"It was Mr. Mycroft Holmes," she said barely above a whisper as if she were apprehensive she'd be overheard. "He was the one who told me not to speak to you about..."

Watson looked into Mrs. Hudson's eyes and could see she was being tortured from within over how to handle this moment.

"He came here only a couple of days ago," she continued. "He wanted assurance the rooms were being kept. Believe me when I tell you, Dr. Watson, this was the first time I'd ever met the man."

"What did he want?" Watson asked.

"He was dropping off the payment for April's rent which was strange because it had always been sent by messenger, and he wanted to know if I had a spare key for your old rooms. I told him I did and I asked him if he wanted to see the rooms he'd been paying for. He said no. All he wanted was the key."

"Did you provide it for him?"

Mrs. Hudson nodded. "I saw no reason not to give it to him. He was paying the rent. Lawfully, it was his."

"And he took it?"

"Yes."

"So now the rooms cannot be examined?" Watson asked.

"Nor cleaned," Mrs. Hudson added.

"Why were you instructed not to tell me of this?"

"I don't know," she said with a shrugging of her shoulders and honesty in her eyes.

Watson sat back in his chair and took a sip from his tea cup. Mrs. Hudson stared at him as he contemplated the bit of information she'd given him.

"Why do you suppose he wanted the extra key?" Watson asked.

"I don't know, Doctor," she said. "I assume to give to someone. Or perhaps to keep someone out."

"That's my thought," Watson said and fell back into

concentration.

Watson took a sip from his tea cup and stood suddenly causing Mrs. Hudson to become slightly startled.

"Mrs. Hudson," Watson said. "I'm sorry for my actions here today. It was wrong of me to accuse you of anything improper or to assume you would in any way conspire against me. I hope you will forgive my inappropriate actions here today."

Mrs. Hudson stood and smiled at her former tenant.

"Nothing to be forgiven for, Doctor," she said.

"You are a wonderful woman," Watson said and smiled at her in return. "I promise when this is all over, I will stop by for a proper visit."

Then, quite unexpectedly, Watson embraced Mrs. Hudson and held her for just a few tender moments.

"You're going to be all right, Dr. Watson," she said with tears in her eyes. "Everything will get better. You'll see."

Dr. Watson nodded and taking his hat, he left the familiar rooms at 221B.

On the street outside of the residence Watson hailed the first cab that came along ignoring the rule Holmes had instilled in him years before.

"The Diogenes Club," Watson told the driver and they were off toward the heart of London.

Chapter Twenty-Six

The cab deposited Dr. Watson at the entrance to the Diogenes Club where Watson paid and tipped the driver without noticing he'd been followed from his old rooms in Baker Street by another cab with a driver whose face was obscured by a scarf.

Watson stomped up the stairs and burst through the doors to the unorthodox club where he loudly demanded the immediate attention of Mycroft Holmes.

"I want to see him, and I want to see him now!" Watson said to the shocked uniformed attendant.

"Sir, if you'll just calm down," the attendant stated in a hushed yet urgent tone in an attempt to quiet Watson's demeanor. "I'm certain we can make arrangements for you."

"I don't want to make arrangements," Watson demanded. "I want to see Mycroft Holmes, and I want to see him this instant. I am not leaving until I do."

"I'm not sure he's even in at the moment, sir," the attendant stated.

"He's in," Watson countered. "He's always in."

"I'm here, Doctor," Mycroft called from across the lobby at the entrance to the Stranger's Room. "Please, come in."

Mycroft stood aside at the entrance until Watson could walk across the lobby to enter the only room in the club that could be used for conversation.

Once inside the Stranger's Room, Mycroft shut the door then turned to Dr. Watson with vehemence in his eyes.

"Dammit, Dr. Watson!" he nearly bellowed. "This has got to stop!"

"Yes," Watson said with nearly the same vitriol. "I am

sick of the lies and the manipulations. You owe me the truth, and by God I will have it."

"You will have what I feel necessary to give you," Mycroft said his anger rising. "I cannot seem to penetrate that granite block you call a head and make you aware of the danger you've placed yourself in as well as a number of my agents. We put you in the Northumberland. You should have remained there. Would it be better for you to have a cell at Scotland Yard until this matter is concluded?"

"Anything would be better than to feel you've been lying to me and placating me. There is no plot to overthrow the American government. Is there? Ronald Adair is NOT a British spy. What is really happening here? Is your brother alive? Tell me the damn truth, you miserable bastard!"

Mycroft Holmes was stunned by this incredible display of bravery. Never in all of his career had he been spoken to in such a matter. It was completely unanticipated and thus, Mycroft was thrown off guard. He was at a loss as to how to immediately respond.

So, Mycroft decided to respond honestly and he took a deep breath.

"My apologies, Dr. Watson," he said with calm and sincerity. "I am unable to tell you anything about what you're involved in. I thought if I could appeal to your sense of national pride, you'd step aside and let Her Majesty's Government handle this matter. However, I can see that is not going to be the case. So, I am very sorry, but I can tell you nothing."

"Your brother is still alive," Watson said in a normal tone but not without accusation. "Isn't he?"

Mycroft stood silently for a moment, "I cannot say one

way or another. As you know, no body was found at Reichenbach."

"That's as good as a yes, to me," Watson said with a satisfied smirk.

"I would hate for you to have to go through his loss for a second time, Doctor," Mycroft said compassionately. "But you believe what you want. I am finished attempting to change your mind."

"Then I choose to believe he is alive, and I will not rest until I prove it," Watson said.

"As you wish," Mycroft said. "You have been checked out of the rooms at the Northumberland. Your bags will be waiting for you at the front desk. You are free to pursue any investigation you feel is necessary, but you will get no more assistance from this office. And if you are found to be a hindrance to any current investigation, I will personally see to it you are thrown in jail until such a time as it will be impossible for you to hinder us any longer, no matter how long that may take. Have I made myself clear to you?"

Watson stood silently.

"That's as good as a yes, to me," Mycroft said and opened the door to the Stranger's Room.

Watson stormed out of the room and crossed to the entrance where he exited slamming the door behind him.

Again, he flagged down the first cab that came his way, once again completely ignoring the safety measure Sherlock Holmes had taught him so long ago.

"Drive," he told the cabby.

"Any special direction, guvnor?" the cabby asked.

"None yet," Watson said fuming. "I need to think for a

bit. Don't worry about the fare. Just drive."

The cabby whipped up his horse and pulled away from the Diogenes Club.

Chapter Twenty-Seven

As the cab drove along the streets of London, Watson contemplated his circumstances. How had he come to this level of confusion? How would Holmes have handled this matter? Why couldn't he get his mind to work the way Holmes's did? "You know my methods, Watson," Holmes used to say. "Apply them." **(26)** So easy for him, he'd been using those methods for decades. It was second nature for him, but for Watson it was tantamount to climbing Mount Everest. And yet, was that actually true? Everest had yet to be climbed but people did climb and explore mountain ranges. It was only a matter of time before the challenge would be met. Watson had seen Holmes use his powers of observation and reasoning countless times. Surely, it could be duplicated. This was not out of the realm of possibility.

Watson took a deep breath and cleared his mind. He quelled the anger he felt boiling within him. He forced himself to calm down and relax so his thoughts would be clear and logical. Slowly he regained control of his emotions and his mind, free of the trappings and cloudiness that comes from making decisions compromised by emotional thinking, began to see matters differently.

"Cabby!" Watson said with sudden realization. "Take me to the two hundred block of Baker Street."

"Right, Guv'nor," the cabby said and made a one hundred eighty degree turn in the street in order to drive toward Baker Street.

Twenty minutes later, Watson was back on Baker Street and approaching 221B. He realized he'd been attacking the problem from the wrong direction. He was desperately trying to find someone who could corroborate his belief that Sherlock Holmes was still alive. In fact, what he should have been doing was trying to prove the fact himself. Keeping an eye on 221B Baker Street would eventually reveal the evidence he needed or prove his theory in error.

"Any particular place you want me to stop?" the cabby asked looking between both sides of the residential street.

"Yes, drive around the corner to the street opposite and stop when I tell you," Watson answered.

The driver did as instructed and when he reached a spot on the opposite street Watson indicated for him to stop.

"Here's good," Watson said and the cabby pulled his horse and hansom to the curb about mid-block from the corner.

"You realize we been followed, guv'nor?" the cabby said as he took a very welcome fare and tip from Dr. Watson.

"I did not," Watson stated. "But it makes no never mind."

Watson dismissed the cabby and caught a glimpse in the gathering darkness of the evening at a four-wheeler and a driver with a scarf covering his face just pulling to the side of the street near the corner he'd just rounded.

Watson immediately ran between two houses and through an alley way. He tried to guess which house was the one directly across the street from 221B Baker Street. He'd taken note of the roof of the building during his pass along Baker Street but with the growing darkness it was becoming difficult to ascertain which building was the one that interested him. Then he noticed the house and recognized the unique roof configuration.

Camden House.

It had stood empty for years ever since Holmes solved a simple case of government blackmail that incarcerated the property owner. An adventure Watson had not written down because it had taken Holmes all of twenty minutes to solve. Still, the fact the criminal was within shouting distance of Holmes's own residence was intriguing and the way the crime was solved appeared almost magical in its swiftness.

Silently and stealthily, Watson made his way to the rear entrance of Camden House and was able to force open a window on a small back porch next to the rear door. Quietly he climbed into the house. Once inside he shut the window and looked out on the dark backyard for any sign of the person or persons tailing him. Watson had already ruled out Mycroft Holmes as a possible tail. There was no way someone of that girth was going to be able to navigate the fencing and terrain Watson had just traversed in an attempt to follow him, but he didn't rule out one of Mycroft's minions being assigned to keep an eye on him at any cost. In many ways, Mycroft was similar to Moriarty. He had a literal army at his disposal that could be utilized for all sorts of assignments in the city and probably many points far removed from London...perhaps even, and almost assuredly, outside of England.

Watson surveilled the back yard and alley way for a few minutes until he was certain no one was in pursuit. He noticed no movement in the gathering gloom but that didn't mean his tail wasn't waiting for complete darkness to follow him.

Positive he'd not been immediately followed, Watson made his way to the front of the house. The main floor windows facing Baker Street were not only shuttered but were also nailed over with boards but Watson had observed earlier the upper two floors had unshuttered windows but there was no way to reach any of them from the outside without being some kind of gymnast or having a ladder easily handy. Slowly, Watson made his way up the dusty staircase to the first floor. From the dirt on the carpeting covering the stairs Watson could see the indentations of at least two different sets of footprints possibly three.

Someone had obviously been in the house since it was made vacant but how recently, Watson could not tell.

On the first floor, Watson followed the footprints to a room that looked out over Baker Street. In fact, the windows in the room looked directly across at the rooms he shared with Sherlock Holmes. It was the perfect vantage point to observe the comings and goings at 221B without being seen from the street.

The room had recently been occupied.

There was a table and three chairs near enough to the window for the gas lamps outside to offer a bit of light. The table had a deck of cards and the remnants of a devoured meal; some kind of sandwich, resting upon it. There were also two cups each with a slight amount of a dried dark liquid remaining in the bottom of each cup, probably coffee judging by the faint aroma. There was very little dust on the table leading Watson to deduce it hadn't been there long enough to gather any and so had to have been utilized within the past week or so. Two of the chairs were situated around the table and the third was positioned back away from the window near a closet that was missing its door but currently had a curtain covering its interior.

The floor was covered with dust that had been quite disturbed by many feet traversing it as if whoever had occupied the room had done so with a great amount of pacing. However, Watson observed the footprints that corresponded to the chair near the closet appeared to have been kept docile for some reason. Whoever made those prints had spent a lot of time in the chair.

"Was this person some kind of prisoner?" Watson wondered.

Taking one of the chairs from the table, Watson positioned it so he could see out the window onto Baker Street but remain mostly in the darkness of the room and unseen by anyone who might be watching from the outside.

If Holmes were indeed alive as Watson had surmised, this was going to be a perfect vantage spot to view his rooms at 221B. He would have a complete view of his old rooms and the street below as well as one of the corners down the block. Any street traffic leading to his old address would easily be observed. If Sherlock Holmes returned, Watson would see him. Now, it was just a matter of how long could he maintain a steady watch.

Chapter Twenty-Eight

The steady watch hadn't gone ten minutes before a four-wheeler pulled to a stop in front of Camden House. The cabby, wearing a dark coat and a scarf across his face quickly climbed down from his perch and darted up the steps to 221B and inside without a knock on the door or a pull of the bell. This appeared to be the same personage who had followed him to the street behind Camden House.

Watson was just getting to his feet when he heard the sound of a door being opened downstairs and what sounded like three or four men storming their way into the building.

"Quiet, you fools," a harsh whisper echoed from downstairs. "You'll make enough noise to raise the dead."

Stealthily, Watson rose from his chair and went to the door of the room.

The men were already climbing the steps still making more noise than should be safe to hide their motions from anyone within the building.

"Ain't nobody in here but us, Clive," one of the intruders remarked. "'Cept for maybe some rats."

The other men chuckled at this claim.

"Shut up about them rats," the one who must have been Clive said with a bit of fear in his voice.

With no way to escape, Watson hid in the former closet and held his breath praying the men would pass this room for another. He reached into his inner jacket pocket and realized too late Mycroft had insisted he leave his Army Webley locked in his desk at his home.

Watson cursed himself for a fool, then held his breath

when he realized the men were entering the very room where he was currently in hiding.

"How'd this chair get here?" Clive asked as he entered the room and walked over to the chair Watson had just recently vacated.

"You musta left it there," the other said. "Whatcha want with this guy?"

"Tie him up like all the other times," Clive said. "In the chair by the closet. Does I gotta spell everything out for you two oafs?"

"We ain't no oafs," a third voice said in a deep but uneducated baritone. "You best stop callin' us names or..."

"Or what, Willie?" Clive said. "You gonna tell the Colonel on me like Petey did? You gonna do that? You remember what happened to Petey, don'tcha?"

"Never mind," Willie said.

"Or maybe yer gonna tell the Inspector here," Clive said and Watson's eyes widened to the size of saucers.

Could it be in his search for Sherlock Holmes he'd been brought the missing Inspector Lestrade?

"That it, Willie?" Clive continued. "You gonna have him arrest me?"

Clive started laughing only not in a booming humorous way. It was more of a sinister, malicious laugh. The laugh of a madman.

"He's all tied up, Clive," the second man said. "And the gag's nice and tight too."

"Good," Clive said. "Who wants to go for something to eat?"

"I ain't got no money," Willie said downhearted.

"Then I guess you get to go," Clive said. "Least you can do for not chippin' in. Right, Nick?"

"Right, Clive," Nick said. "You gotta be good for somethin' Willie."

"I was good for puttin' a fright into that little girl at that Lord's house, weren't I?"

"She wasn't no little girl," Clive said. "She was their cook, is all."

"Yeah," Nick agreed. "Besides there ain't nothing to scarin' somebody. Any one of us coulda done it."

"Okay. Okay. I'll go," Willie conceded. "I ain't gonna make no more trouble. I just ain't got no money for to buy nothin's all."

Nick and Clive tossed some money onto the table.

Willie scooped it up and tucked it into a pocket.

"Where'm I goin'?" Willie asked.

"How 'bout the shop down the street?" Nick asked. "They got good sammiches."

"I was feelin' more toward some fish and chips," Clive said.

"Yeah," Nick agreed, "Fish and chips. Sounds good to me."

"The vendor four blocks from here?" Willie asked disappointed.

"That's right," Clive said. "Problem?"

"Naw," Willie said downhearted. "Just makin' sure."

Willie left the room and could be heard tromping down the stairs and finally out the back door.

Clive took a seat at the table near the window. Nick looked outside before sitting down.

231

"There's a growler out front," Nick said looking down at the four-wheeler.

"Anybody in it?" Clive asked.

"Don't think so. No cabby neither."

"Then don't worry about it."

"Feel like playing some cribbage?" Nick asked taking a seat and removing a deck of cards.

"Naw," Clive answered. "Play with yourself if it suits ya."

Clive laughed at his own wit and Nick began to deal out a hand of solitaire.

Watson breathed a silent sigh of relief.

With Willie gone, the odds were now even if he could free Lestrade from his bonds.

Reaching into his pocket, Watson removed the pen knife he carried and knelt down in the shadows of the closet. This would be the first time he used the knife. It was a noble reason, but he still felt a tiny bit apprehensive in utilizing it. What if it should be broken somehow? It could never be replaced. Fortunately, the reason for using it far outweighed any reason for not using the blade. Slowly, he lifted the curtain until he could see Lestrade's hands tied behind his back.

Expecting a reaction, Watson reached out and grasped one of Lestrade's wrists. Lestrade was startled and jumped in his chair. Watson immediately pulled his hand back and dropped the curtain.

"What's yer problem?" Nick said looking over his shoulder at the bound Inspector.

Lestrade made a movement in his chair to give the impression he was just getting comfortable.

"Best make yerself comfortable," Nick said. "You're gonna be in that chair until the crack o' dawn."

"That copper's all twitchy," Nick continued to Clive.

"It's this place," Clive said. "I hate bein' on Baker Street."

"Why's that? Is it the rats?" Nick chuckled.

"I don't wanna hear no more about them rats," Clive ordered angrily.

"Sorry, Clive," Nick said. "I was just havin' you on."

"It's not the rats. It's not all the dust in this place neither. Don'tcha know what we're lookin' at out there?" Clive said pointing at the window.

Nick shrugged his shoulders.

"That's 221B across the street. Most famous address in all London. It's where Sherlock Holmes lives."

"You mean used to."

"Do I?" asked Clive strangely.

"Yeah," Nick said. "He fell off a cliff or something a few years ago."

"And no one ever found his body."

"That don't mean nothin'. It was a long ways down. He coulda got stuck in a crevice or busted into a million pieces on his way down to the bottom."

"How could someone get busted into a million pieces?"

The two men continued their ridiculous debate while Watson lifted the curtain and began cutting through the rope that bound Inspector Lestrade's hands. Lestrade didn't jump this time when Watson grasped his wrist to let him know he was there. Lestrade even forced his bound hands further behind him to allow Watson easier access to the rope.

Watson worked desperately to free the Inspector while

attempting to block out the conversation of the two men as they described in detail how gruesome a death over a cliff would be and how impossible it would be to survive such a fall.

"What if he never fell?" Clive proffered.

"How could he not've fell?" Nick asked. "His ol' pal that doctor feller, woulda found him and he didn't."

"What if that doctor feller was lyin' about not seeing his friend. Ya know, there's some in the organization what think that doctor is hidin' his old friend."

"What for?"

"So's he can work in secret. Why'd you think we got this copper here?" Clive asked.

Watson stopped cutting through the rope at this moment when he felt Lestrade tense. He realized Lestrade was watching the men and they must have looked in his direction. Lestrade was signaling Watson to stop until it was clear to continue. When it was clear, Lestrade relaxed his wrists and Watson continued to slice through the knotted rope.

A moment later, Watson was through the rope and it slowly began to unravel. Lestrade began to unwind it from his wrists all the while keeping his hands behind him and slowly winding the rope into a tight ball.

"We got the copper because he's bein' used as bait," Clive explained to his slow-witted partner.

"Bait?" Nick asked. "For what?"

"Geez, Nick, ain't you been listenin' to anything I been sayin'? The Colonel thinks ol' Sherlock is still alive and helpin' the police solve crimes. We got this house to hide in to keep an eye on his old digs in case he comes back to his place. This bloke here, though, he couldn't solve the mystery of what he had for breakfast without the help of Sherlock Holmes."

Lestrade stomped his feet.

"Yeah," Clive said to Lestrade. "I'm talking about you. Everybody knows Sherlock Holmes is the brains over at Scotland Yard. You guys couldn't be put in charge of finding lost pets if it weren't for Sherlock Holmes."

Again, Lestrade stomped his feet and glared at Clive.

Clive got up from his seat and crossed the room to where Lestrade sat.

"What's that?" Clive said mocking the Inspector. "You got somethin' you wanna say?"

Lestrade glared at Clive and growled through the gag in his mouth all the while keeping his hands behind his back to keep Clive and Nick under the belief he was incapacitated.

"Cain't hears ya?" Clive said mockingly, cupped his right ear and bent closer to Lestrade's mouth. "Why don'tcha try 'nunciatin'?"

Clive glanced over to Nick who was laughing at his friend's humor, and Lestrade made his move.

He pulled his arms from behind his back, grabbed Clive's head and slammed Clive's skull into his knees with a sickening crack. Clive fell to the floor. Lestrade stood up and delivered another kick to Clive's head knocking it back on his neck in a whiplash movement and rendering him unconscious. Watson, meanwhile, had emerged from the closet. He picked up the chair Lestrade had just vacated and brought it down on a stunned Nick's skull as the thug attempted to stand. Nick went down like a sack of wet garbage and remained on the floor.

Just then, the door downstairs was opened and the plodding footsteps of Willie could be heard clomping their way toward and then up the stairs.

Lestrade waited behind the door to the room and just as Willie appeared, he slammed the door in his face. He and Watson heard a grunt followed by Willie stumbling backward, crashing into the railing outside the door and finally the thundering crash of his body hitting the ground floor below.

A police whistle was heard from immediately outside the front entrance of Camden House. It was followed by three more from different locations in the area.

Lestrade removed the gag from his mouth and tossed it on the floor in disgust.

"Thank you for your help," Lestrade said as he stared at Watson standing in the darkness with the light from the street behind him. Watson moved slightly and the light illuminated his facial features so Inspector Lestrade could recognize him. "Lord be, Dr. Watson!"

"I'm so glad I found you," Watson said.

The two men embraced for a moment each showing an enormous amount of relief.

They separated the moment the front door of Camden House was battered down and they heard the cry of "Police!" from downstairs.

Watson immediately recognized the voice. It was Inspector Gregson. There was a thundering of footsteps as more officers piled through the doorway.

"Up here, Inspector!" Watson called down to the police officer. "I have a surprise for you."

"Dr. Watson?" the inspector called tentatively. "Is that you up there?"

"Yes," Watson replied happily. "And I'm in the presence

of a friend of yours."

Gregson ordered the men who entered with him to secure the scene then quickly climbed the stairs and entered the room. He was carrying a lantern and he shown it first on Watson's face to make sure he was who he said he was then moved the beam over to Inspector Lestrade.

"Lestrade!" he said in a hoarse whisper. It was as if the air in his lungs had been sucked out in shock. "I can't...is it really..."

"It's me, Gregson," Lestrade said covering his emotion better than his counterpart. "Let's not burble about this, shall we?"

"But...how...?"

"Dr. Watson was here to save me," Lestrade said. "I assumed he was working with you."

Both Watson and Gregson shook their heads.

"Then, how did you know to come here?" Lestrade asked of both men.

"We were given a tip that if we came to this address we'd be witness to something that would be invaluable to Scotland Yard. So, men were posted at the corners and the alley. All we saw was the big guy now lying on the floor downstairs come in through the back door. A moment later the ruckus began and the whistles were blowing. Then, the two of you."

Watson and Lestrade followed Gregson out of Camden House while a half dozen constables made use of their handcuffs and shackled the three thugs before escorting them to a waiting police carriage. All had serious injuries but nothing life threatening in the end. They had been beaten and deservedly so. It was discovered that Lestrade had been treated poorly while in their custody. He'd had only two meals during the time of his abduction and barely enough water to keep his thirst at bay.

"I'm going to stay here on Baker Street with Inspector Gregson," Lestrade told Watson when they were back on street level. "I have to brief him on everything I've been through, and then I'll help him tidy up the scene of the crime."

A thought instantly dawned on Watson.

"There might be another!" Watson said jerking his head in the direction of his old rooms at 221B.

"Another what?" Gregson asked suddenly concerned.

"Another member of this gang," Watson said and mentioned the scarved figure he saw race into 221B prior to the arrival of the three thugs and Inspector Lestrade.

"We'll check it out," Lestrade said appearing to take control of the situation. When Gregson opened his mouth to protest, Lestrade placed a gentle hand of restraint on his arm. "We'd better get you clear of this scene, Doctor,

"Shall I meet you at Scotland Yard?" Watson asked eagerly. "I'm willing to provide my statement."

"That won't be necessary tonight," Lestrade said smiling. "Maybe in the morning. I'll have a police carriage take you home."

Watson nodded a bit disappointed.

"Thank you, Doctor," Lestrade said holding out his hand for Watson to shake.

"My pleasure," Watson said and grasped his friend's hand.

They shook firmly.

Gregson signaled the driver of a police prisoner wagon, then took Watson over to the carriage while Lestrade took another constable and headed toward 221B.

"Take Dr. Watson here to his home in Kensington, will you, constable?" Gregson said.

"Certainly, Inspector," the constable said. "Hop on up, Doctor. Won't do no good to have you getting out of the back of this heap with all your neighbors watchin'."

Watson smiled and climbed up next to the constable.

"I will see you gentlemen soon," Watson said.

"That you will, Doctor," Gregson answered and gave a slight salute.

The constable whipped up his horses and slowly made his way through the confusion on Baker Street.

"Right exciting, that," the constable said. "How'd you figure it?"

"Figure what?" Watson asked.

"Figure where they was keepin' the Inspector?"

"Oh," Watson said with a chuckle. "I didn't."

"You didn't? Then what was ya doin' here tonight?"

"Constable, it was all blind luck," Watson said as they neared the corner at the end of Baker Street. "I was looking for Sherlock Holmes."

As they rounded the corner, Watson looked back toward his police friends and noticed they were talking to the tall, cloaked figure with a the scarf wrapped around his face he'd seen run into his former boarding house. As he adjusted his seating to get a better view, the carriage passed around the corner and out of sight of 221B and Camden House.

"But, ain't Sherlock Holmes dead, Doctor?" the constable asked with a bit of melancholy.

"Yes," Watson said with heavy sadness as he realized his

deductions while instrumental in the rescue of Inspector Lestrade, were entirely wrong when it came to his great friend. "Yes, he's dead."

Chapter Twenty-Nine

It would be a full week before Dr. John Watson and Inspector Gerard Lestrade would finally be able to meet for dinner. They had chosen Simpson's for their repast and the two bickered over who would take up the bill.

"I'm thanking you," Lestrade argued genially. "You saved my life, Doctor. This is the least I can do."

"And you've been through a horrendous ordeal," Watson countered. "This is the least *I* can do."

In the end, the two decided on separate checks and paid for each other's meal.

"A delightful evening, Doctor," Lestrade said. "Once the matter of the check was decided."

"Indeed," Watson said and laughed pleasantly along with the Inspector.

The waiter poured each of them a cup of coffee.

"Anything for dessert, gentlemen?" he asked. "We have a wonderful pastry selection available this evening."

"Nothing for me," Watson said. "Lestrade?"

"I couldn't eat another bite," the Inspector said.

Before leaving, the waiter placed a box of matches on the table should either man decide on an after dinner cigar. Neither did.

"So," Watson said a bit apprehensively. "How was it?"

"Delicious," Lestrade said with a grin. "I thought I'd made that clear."

"You know what I mean."

"The abduction," Lestrade acquiesced and his demeanor changed instantly.

Watson nodded showing concern.

"It wasn't pleasant," Lestrade said with a wry smile.

Watson nodded again.

"They didn't beat me or anything," the Inspector continued and drew in a deep breath. "It was more as though I was some kind of inconvenience to them. Having to transport me someplace new every day. Four different locations in total. I never even knew Baker Street was one of them until that final night. They kept my head covered with some kind of cloth bag whenever I was being moved and removed it once I was inside whatever destination they'd dragged me to."

"What *did* they do to you?" Watson asked.

"Ignored me, mostly," Lestrade said trying to make it sound like as if it were nothing more than a trifle. "I had to remind them if I wanted to get a drink of water and when that was provided they'd remove the gag from my mouth. Food was a luxury. I think I've lost fifteen pounds since this started. They generally only had food for themselves. It wasn't anything like what we just had, but when you're hungry, everything looks like a feast."

"Was it the same three men every time?"

"Mainly. I think there might have been a time or two when someone else was involved."

"Why'd they do it?" Watson asked. "Why'd they kidnap you?"

Lestrade thought for a moment.

"I'm not certain," he said. "Something's afoot. I heard them say things about a colonel and how he was rebuilding the organization. I also caught fragments of conversation that led me to believe this colonel was cheating at some kind of game, probably cards."

"That doesn't seem to be any reason to kidnap a police inspector," Watson said.

"Not at all," Lestrade agreed.

"A colonel, you say," Watson said thoughtfully.

"Yes, but nothing further."

"Mycroft Holmes said something about a Colonel Moran they were keeping an eye on in regards to the old Moriarty gang. That's probably him. Don't you think?"

"Could be. Everyone arrested that night has stayed silent about the whole business," Lestrade said. "Very tight-lipped these lads. Reminds me of the old Moriarty gang and how none of them would turn on the old Professor."

"They mentioned Sherlock Holmes when we were in Camden House," Watson said.

"Yes," Lestrade said and suddenly had to clear his throat. "I heard that too. They were under some belief our old friend was...still alive."

Watson smiled sheepishly.

"You too?" Lestrade said.

"I'm afraid so," Watson answered. "I was almost absolutely certain Holmes was living back at Baker Street or would very soon arrive, and I was going to watch until my suspicions were satisfied one way or another."

"How long were you prepared to remain in Camden House?"

"I must admit that part of my plan was not that well thought out. I had no provisions for a lengthy stay. Luckily, I didn't have to remain too long."

"Luckily for me too."

"The incident at the Fairchild house," Watson said getting back to the original story.

"Ah," Lestrade said. "That was staged to get me to investigate and thus put me in a position to be abducted."

"So, the Fairchilds were never in any danger?"

"None, as far as I can tell."

"They should be greatly relieved," Watson said.

"They were," Lestrade said. "I informed them myself. Oh, and you'll be happy to know that young constable Evert and Lydia Caine appear to be an item."

"That's wonderful," Watson said with a smile.

"Not for the Fairchilds," Lestrade said. "If things work out, Miss Caine will probably leave their employ to take care of her new husband. They'll have to find another cook and from what I've been told, she will be a difficult bill to fill."

"Well, pass along my good wishes to young Evert when you see him," Watson said.

"I will and I'll be seeing him a great deal over the next few months. Seems he has ambition."

"Wants to be an inspector," Watson said.

"Yes," Lestrade agreed. "Plans on passing over any rank promotions so he can do it as quickly as possible. Wants to be the youngest inspector in Scotland Yard history."

"Think he can do it?"

"Well, he has the drive. Seems he has the intelligence. Wants me to mentor him. That should count for something."

"He'd be learning from one of the best," Watson said finishing off his coffee.

"Thank you, Doctor," Lestrade said with a slight blush. "I wish that were true."

"It is," Watson countered. "Holmes called you 'the best of a bad lot.' **(27)** I know that doesn't sound like much of a complement but for him it was."

"So, that brings me to a question," Lestrade said. "How did you come to the conclusion that Sherlock Holmes was still among the living?"

"I'm afraid, I had made a series of deductions that led me to that belief. It was quite erroneous."

Watson went on tell the Inspector all of the clues that led him to believe Holmes had somehow survived the incident at the Reichenbach Falls three years earlier.

Lestrade looked stunned and a bit nervous.

"Are you all right, Inspector?" Watson asked suddenly concerned for his friend.

"Yes, yes," Lestrade said instantly regaining his composure.

"Well, I can certainly see your logic," Lestrade continued in a kind of dismissive tone as he rose from his seat. "I'd like to thank you again for a delightful evening, Doctor, but I really must be on my way. There is still a great deal of work to be done in unraveling the events of the last few days and I have to get my rest before work tomorrow."

Watson stood as well and shook the Inspector's offered hand.

However, as Watson was about to release his hand, Lestrade suddenly grabbed it with intensity.

"You are a good friend, Doctor," he said mysteriously. "Better days are coming. I can't go into any more detail at this time, but just know that...better days are coming."

Lestrade released Dr. Watson's hand and immediately left

245

the restaurant.

Watson stood silently for a moment before retaking his seat. He'd been stunned by the inspector's final remarks. What could he have meant?

* * *

The next morning was warm and filled with sunshine.

Watson took a cab to the cemetery where he knelt at Mary's grave site.

"He's safe, Mary," Watson told his wife. "I saved Inspector Lestrade. I couldn't have done it without you. You made me a better man; a stronger man. I wish you were here with me now."

A tear fell from Watson's face as he placed another bouquet of flowers against his wife's headstone.

Watson stood.

"I'll see you soon," he said as he gently patted the grave marker and recalled his wife's memory. "I love you."

Watson looked around at the hundreds of other headstones. He knew none of the people who were buried there and probably none of the visitors who came every day, but he did know one thing.

There was a headstone missing.

A memorial not yet erected.

One honoring his great friend, Sherlock Holmes.

Would it be a good idea to have one placed at an obviously empty grave site? Would it be presumptuous of him to do it when it should fall on Mycroft Holmes to be responsible?

Better days were coming, Lestrade had said.

Perhaps it would be prudent to wait for those days before making that decision.

Watson left the cemetery.

* * *

Better days, Watson thought as he exited the cab he'd hailed from the cemetery and which had deposited him in front of his home. He paid the cabby and was about to turn to his steps when a voice behind him called him by name.

"Dr. Watson?"

Watson turned and saw it was young Alfie from the Northumberland Hotel. He had shed his hotel uniform and was now wearing the uniform of a telegram delivery boy.

"Alfie!" Watson said, then indicated Alfie's new clothing. "What's all this?"

"New job, Doctor," Alfie said. "Better pay. Gets me outdoors. Gives me exercise. Helps me learn the city. And the tips ain't bad neither."

"Good for you, lad," Watson said with a genuine grin. "Good for you."

"Got a telegram for you, sir," he said fishing the envelope out of his satchel.

"You do?" Watson said taking the telegram from the youth.

Watson opened it and saw it was from Inspector Lestrade.

"Ronald Adair murdered. Would appreciate your assistance on Park Lane. Lestrade." it read.

"Oh, this is terrible," Watson said.

"Bad news, sir?" Alfie asked.

"Yes," Watson said but would share no more. "I have to go, Alfie, but promise me you'll stop by now and again and let me know of your adventures."

"I will, Doctor," Alfie said with a smile.

Watson hailed another cab and in a moment was on his way to Park Lane to meet with Inspector Lestrade.

Epilogue

Mycroft Holmes sat at a large table in the currently empty Stranger's Room of the Diogenes Club. In front of him were the remains of a small snack and a number of well-thumbed newspapers all folded open to stories involving a mysterious shooting on Park Lane.

The door to the Stranger's Room opened and a tall, gaunt figure in a long coat and a scarf covering his face was ushered in without fanfare or introduction.

"You've heard, I take it," Mycroft said to the figure and made a slight indication toward the newspapers.

"Of Adair's demise? Yes," the figure responded after glancing at the papers. "Tragic, but not entirely unexpected."

"Are you of the belief Colonel Moran was involved?"

"I have little doubt. Cheating at cards was just one of the

many ways of his continued funding of the late Professor's criminal enterprise."

"Well, I'm positive of it."

"Do you think Watson is in danger?" the figure asked with great concern.

"I am positive of that as well," Mycroft said with certainty.

"Then it's time he knew the whole truth and, quite possibly, the full reasoning behind why he was kept in the dark for so long," the shadowy figure stated removing his coat and scarf to reveal his high forehead, hawk-like nose and gray eyes.

"Not too good an idea you sending him those cryptic missives," Mycroft admonished. "They kept him on a trail I would much rather he'd stayed clear of."

"You were aware of those?"

"The Good Doctor showed one to me. I figured there had to be others. You were...preparing him, I gather."

"In a subtle sort of manner."

"Not all that subtle," Mycroft said with a rare half smile.

"Well, in informing him, I'm not so certain Watson needs to know all of the details," Mycroft continued. "There are some State secrets involved in the reasons for your disappearance."

"Perhaps you're right," the figure conceded.

"How do you think the Good Doctor will react to the news?" Mycroft asked.

"I wouldn't be surprised if he fainted," was the figure's response.

"Then, be careful, dear brother," Mycroft said. "His heart is certainly stout, but the sight of you back from a watery grave might be too much for him to handle. Especially after what I had to put him through to deny your existence and in contrary to your 'planted' evidence."

"Then I shall present myself to him in disguise; an elderly bibliophile, I think."

"A good choice," Mycroft said and stood from his seat. "And the sooner, the better in this matter. Have Lestrade send for him."

The figure nodded in agreement.

Mycroft escorted the shadowy figure to the door.

"Welcome back, Sherlock," Mycroft said to his brother as he opened the door to the Stranger's Room.

"It is certainly wonderful to be back," Sherlock Holmes said with a rare smile.

Then, with a flourish, Sherlock Holmes added "The game is, at last, afoot."

Without another word, Sherlock Holmes left the

Strangers' Room and the Diogenes Club to seek out his dear friend and begin another adventure.

The End

Annotations

1. THE SIGN OF FOUR was the second Sherlock Holmes adventure to see print. It was commissioned along with Oscar Wilde's THE PICTURE OF DORIAN GRAY. SIGN told the story of Mary Morstan (who would later become Watson's wife) who'd been receiving a strange

package of a lustrous pearl each year on her birthday. When she received a note claiming she'd been a "wronged woman," she went to Sherlock Holmes for assistance on what to do and there she met Dr. Watson, the man who would become her husband.

2. THE FINAL PROBLEM was the last short story published in the Strand Magazine in the nineteenth century and detailed how Holmes had come to be attacked by some of his arch foe, Professor Moriarty's, men after he'd smashed the criminal mastermind's organization. Holmes and Watson fled to Switzerland in an attempt to dodge Moriarty, but Moriarty followed them and in a final confrontation between the "best and wisest" man Watson had ever know and the "Napoleon of crime" the two were sent hurtling over the cliffs to their deaths in the roiling waters of the Reichenbach Falls.

3. A STUDY IN SCARLET first appeared in Beeton's Christmas Annual in 1887 and was the first detailed adventure of Sherlock Holmes.

4. Inspector Tobias Gregson was first introduced in the novel A Study in Scarlet along with Inspector Lestrade. Holmes described these two Scotland Yarders as "the best of a bad lot."

5. The case investigated in A STUDY IN SCARLET.

6. Here Gregson is presumably speaking of Athelney Jones and Stanley Hopkins. Athelney Jones first appeared in THE SIGN OF FOUR to investigate the murder of Bartholomew Sholto. However, an Inspector Peter Jones assisted in capturing John Clay in THE ADVENTURE OR THE RED-HEADED LEAGUE. Without a first

name it can't be clear who's being mentioned. Stanley Hopkins worked with Holmes in THE ABBEY GRANGE, BLACK PETER, and THE GOLDEN PINCE-NEZ. He was a young man to have achieved the rank of Inspector and Holmes had high hopes for him.

7. THE FINAL PROBLEM.

8. In A SCANDAL IN BOHEMIA the first short adventure of Sherlock Holmes published in the Strand Magazine, Holmes tests Watson's powers of observation by asking him how many steps lead up to their flat. Holmes states Watson has climbed them any number of times so he surely knows the number of them. But Watson is unaware proving Holmes statement "You see but you do not observe."

9. A SCANDAL IN BOHEMIA.

10. The University of Westminster, I'm assuming.

11. THE FINAL PROBLEM

12. Mycroft Holmes was Sherlock's older and more intelligent brother. He was introduced in THE ADVENTURE OF THE GREEK INTERPRETER.

13. THE SIGN OF FOUR

14. From THE SIX NAPOLEONS "The Press, Watson, is a most valuable institution, if you only know how to use it." Seems Holmes was manipulating reporters long before Watson mentioned it in this later adventure.

15. From THE GREEK INTERPRETER where Watson is first informed of Sherlock's older and more intelligent brother.

16. Also from THE GREEK INTERPRETER where Mycroft talked about watching and studying humanity from the

window. He and his brother then put on a show of deductive reasoning and observation about a man standing on the street corner. The wittiness of it leads the reader to believe the two brothers often did this to amuse themselves.

17. Sherlock Holmes uses this phrase himself in A SCANDAL IN BOHEMIA when he is able to deduce the identity of a masked stranger who has come to him for assistance.

18. Sherlock Holmes uses this phrase in THE BLUE CARBUNCLE.

19. From THE FINAL PROBLEM where Watson first learns of the existence of Professor James Moriarty and his evil empire.

20. The U.S. Marshal's Service was often used to protect the President of the United States prior to the creation of the U.S. Secret Service (which, itself, was originally created to investigate cases of counterfeiting before taking on the additional task of protecting the president). Ward Hill Lamon was the personal body guard for President Lincoln and was a U.S. Marshal.

21. The term "Private Eye" originated with the Pinkerton Detective Agency which was created by Allan Pinkerton, a Scottish detective and spy, and Edward Rucker, a Chicago attorney. They called the firm the North-Western Police Agency but it was later changed to The Pinkerton Detective Agency. Their motto was "We Never Sleep" and the logo had an unblinking eye displayed on it. Since they were a private firm, they became known as "Private Eyes." The term also might originate from the

simple term of P.I. for Private Investigator.

22. Alfie is referring to Sir Henry Baskerville who stayed at the Northumberland Hotel and was the victim of a strange crime when one of his new boots was stolen from outside his room (boots were often left outside a room to be polished). The boot was located soon after and then one of his old black boots was stolen. This clue would be very important to Holmes in solving the case.

23. This instruction was first given to Dr. Watson by Sherlock Holmes in The Adventure of the Final Problem. Holmes was telling Watson how not to be followed and how to get to the train station to meet him in the morning.

24. Dr. Watson is undoubtedly speaking of Sir Arthur Conan Doyle who is credited with the release of the Sherlock Holmes stories for publication. Sir Arthur was a doctor first specializing in problems of the eye. By this time, he'd already moved to London to set up practice and was no longer in Edinburgh, Scotland, his homeland.

25. This is probably the most famous quote attributed to Sherlock Holmes (outside of "Elementary, my dear Watson" which was never said in the original sixty Sherlock Holmes stories). It comes from The Sign of Four.

26. This is from the first Chapter of THE HOUND OF THE BASKERVILLES where Holmes offers Watson a walking stick left behind by a potential client and asks him to recreate the owner based on his observations of the cane.

27. This description of the Scotland Yarders Lestrade and Gregson is from A STUDY IN SCARLET and was

mentioned by Holmes upon his arrival at Number 3 Lauriston Gardens where their first adventure would begin.

Acknowledgements

This book would not exist without the help of certain individuals who have assisted me even long before I ever set pen to paper.

Of course there is Sir Arthur Conan Doyle, the creator of Sherlock Holmes and Dr. John H. Watson. Now, there is Mr. Steve Emecz and Ms. Nicko Vaughn De Wheel of MX Publishing and Orange Pip Books who are keeping the Great Detective and the Good Doctor alive. I thank them for their great assistance and guidance in improving this manuscript.

Mr. Mort Castle, great writer and greater friend, who put up with me before I'd ever sold a single word of my own writing.

Two great teachers; Mr. Thomas B. Scarth, who introduced me to the great joy of reading which then resulted in the great misery (?) of writing and Pamela (Holck) Ryan, who saw absolutely no talent in my acting, but encouraged my creativity in writing for the stage, performing improvisation and appreciating Theater Arts.

Mr. Dan Sugrue and Mr. Nick DiGilio of WGN Radio in Chicago who made my obsession with all things Sherlock look like I was pretty cool.

Also, some really good friends who are no longer around for me to thank personally; Jerry Williamson, David B. Silva, Eugene Izzi and the best friend anyone could ever ask for...Thomas W. Krueger. We shared many adventures together. I was proud to be his Watson.

Finally, to the best daughter a father could dream of having; Sarah, who once told me I broke her heart with one of my horror stories thus getting me back to writing mystery fiction. I love you.

Also from Orange Pip Books

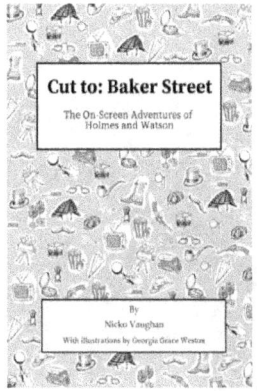

It is well documented that Sherlock Holmes is the most depicted literary character on screen; he even has an entry in the Guinness Book of Records to prove it. This reference guide covers depictions of the world's most famous detective, and his faithful companion, from the first silent film Sherlock Holmes is Baffled (1900) to the Will Ferrell, John C. Reilly comedy Holmes and Watson (2018).

As well as cinema and television portrayals, this book by Nicko Vaughan (Author of The Wordy Companion: An A-Z Guide to Sherlockian Phraseology) also covers documentaries, animations and web series adaptations alongside début feature artwork by graphic artist Georgia Grace Weston.

Combining encyclopaedia, biography and reference structure, this book comprehensively explores the many celluloid faces, cathode-ray shapes and digital sizes of Sherlock Holmes and Doctor John Watson, so far.

Also from Orange Pip Books

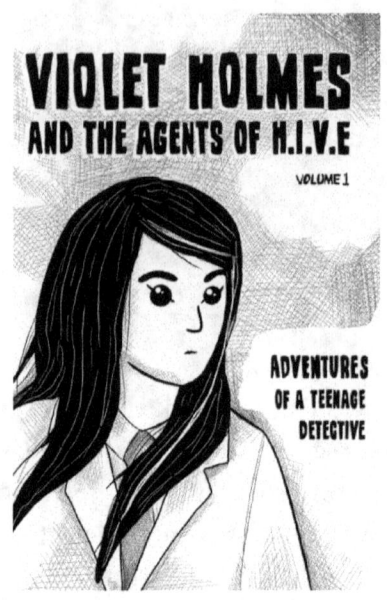

Violet Holmes is not an ordinary teenager because, well, nothing is ordinary when you're the adopted daughter of the great Sherlock Holmes. Having been home schooled for her entire life she has decided to take the plunge, at 14, and attend Bardle Secondary School to study for her exams. But after a week, she notices that the school hides a deep secret, and she's determined to crack it wide open. Are the current spate of school thefts the work of criminal masterminds? Is there really a secret society behind closed doors? Can a girl like Violet make friends and fit in?